THE OTHER SIDE
OF SILENCE

Richard Dew

Richard Dew

ISBN: 1974476308
ISBN-13: 9781974476305
Library of Congress Control Number: 2017912766
CreateSpace Independent Publishing Platform
North Charleston, South Carolina

If we had a keen vision and feeling of all ordinary human life, it would be like hearing the grass grow and the squirrel's heart beat, and we should die of that roar which lies on the other side of silence.

—George Eliot (Mary Ann Evans)

CHAPTER ONE

He gazed out at the eager faces of the students clad in their crisp white jackets. They're so young, so innocent. They have no idea of what it took to be a physician. No idea of the emotional and physical toll the grind ahead of them would exact. No idea a significant number of them would not be present four years hence. No idea of what it had cost him to reach this, his ultimate goal.

Dr. Rosman finished his introduction. "I give you the new dean of the Macmillan Medical School, Dr. Luke Brady."

After brief applause, two hundred eyes fixed on him. Two hundred hands poised, ready to enter his every word.

Luke rose and stepped forward—two inches over six feet, lean from daily jogging, gray hair cropped short, spotless white lab coat. He looked the way a physician was supposed to look.

"I'm Dr. Luke Brady. On behalf of the staff and administration, I welcome you. You have labored long and hard to get here. I assure you, the next four years will be longer and harder." He gave a reassuring smile. "But I promise you, it will be the most stimulating and rewarding time of your life."

The room was silent.

"Medicine is a noble calling. Our goal is to help those who hurt, to console those who grieve, and to lift up those who have fallen. We are allowed where even priests cannot go. We must not take this trust lightly."

He noted the curly-haired student, fifth row, third seat from the left, roll his eyes and begin texting.

"I want to read to you some excerpts from an article I read recently.

"'Into whatever houses I enter, I will go into them for the benefit of the sick…I will follow that method of treatment which according to my ability and judgment, I consider for the benefit of my patients…Whatever in connection with my professional practice I see or hear in the lives of men which ought not be spoken abroad, I will not divulge…With purity and with holiness I will pass my life and practice my art.'

"Does anyone know the source of this quotation?" He pointed to the texter. "How about you, Mr.…?"

"Parker…sir, Henry Parker," he stammered, frantically fumbling to make his phone disappear.

"Who said that, Mr. Parker?"

"I don't know, sir," Parker said in desperation as his phone clattered to the floor.

Luke scanned the class. "Anyone care to hazard a guess?"

The students shifted in their seats and stared at their laptops, avoiding eye contact. Finally, a tall blond female in the fourth row raised her hand.

"Yes?"

"I think that's part of the Hippocratic oath."

"Right!" he said as they gave a collective groan. "Give the lady a Kewpie doll."

He let them quiet. "There's one other part of the oath. I want you to get this one verbatim. Don't ever forget it."

Fingers again hovered over keyboards.

"In no uncertain terms, Hippocrates says, 'I will reckon him who taught me this art dear to me as my parents; to share my substance with him and to relieve his necessities if required.'"

He gave them a puckish smile. "Remember that when I hit you up for a beer."

They laughed and relaxed.

"Seriously," he continued, "this was written twenty-five hundred years ago and is still applicable today. Hippocrates recognized, as we must, the patient comes first." He repeated more slowly, emphasizing each word, "The patient comes first. It's not about me, it's not about you, it's not about the insurance company, it's not about the government—it's about the patient. Without patients, we are of no use."

He paused and let this sink in. "When you leave Macmillan Medical School, you will be endowed with one thing for certain—competence. You will be competent physicians, or you will not graduate. Mediocrity is not an option. I hope each of you develops two equally important attributes: caring and compassion. Always remember, patients are just as interested in how much you care as in how much you know. We will do our very best to teach caring and compassion by example, but for the most part, these are up to you. For some of you, they will almost be second nature. Others will develop them by conscious, repeated effort and practice. An unfortunate few, either because of psychological makeup or deliberate decision, will never acquire them. This is a tragedy, for they will miss the most rewarding aspect of medicine."

He hesitated, shook his head, and swallowed several times.

"As you...As you...As you..." His smooth delivery became a stammer. He grasped the podium. His vision became fuzzy; loud buzzing and excruciating pain filled his head. Then everything went black, and he collapsed, convulsing to the floor.

CHAPTER TWO

Darkness. Floating. Then a barely recognizable blur. Like watching a chaotic home movie, silent save for a continuous, loud hum. Disconnected, random single frames or short snippets: a barefoot, towheaded boy, running across a meadow, him at age twelve, fishing with his dad, him sinking a long-jump shot, a small boy casting lures from the bank of a pond, him kissing his bride, him walking the familiar halls of City Hospital, him sitting on the end of a dock, feet dangling in the water. The hum crescendos into a shrill buzz. A giant fish, black with glowing red eyes and huge piranha teeth, grabs him by the leg and jerks him into the water. "God, no, I didn't mean for it to happen!" His scream dies with a gurgle.

Like a continuous, repeating loop, bits and pieces play and re-play, always ending with the terrifying fish dragging him under.

⊸⊱⊰⊸

Darkness...floating again...fewer flickers...fewer repeats...darkness fading...gray...humming gone...other noises...far off.

Without warning, the background stir swelled, and Luke was bathed with dazzling light. He blinked, and his gaze gradually adapted to the sudden glare. He recognized the familiar sights and sounds of the ICU. Medical personnel scurried around like so many ants, pausing here to relay a bit of information or there to receive a rapid report, then rushing on. As a nurse stepped back from recording vital signs, a phlebotomist smoothly slipped in to leech blood into red-, green-, yellow-, and purple-topped tubes. A pharmacy assistant maneuvered his cart of medications into the drug room just before a dietary aide wheeled her six-foot-tall pushcart bearing twenty covered trays of food. Nurses changed IV bags, suctioned endotracheal tubes, placed or removed bedpans, and gave injections.

No carts collided. No one bumped into another. This hodgepodge of seemingly random activity functioned efficiently, as if synchronized by an unseen choreographer.

Sounds were muted but ever present: hushed conversations, the whir as a monitor regurgitated a long strip of EKG squiggles, the soft moan of a semicomatose patient. From time to time, the blare of an alarm signaled a catastrophic emergency or merely a loose monitor pad.

To his left, Lauren Levin, his favorite ICU nurse, sat at the keyboard on the nurses' desk. She was not only a superb nurse but also shared his skewed sense of humor. They competed to see who could create the worst puns and limericks. She spun around as he struggled to sit up.

"Whoa," she said and pulled him up, adjusted his pillow, and raised the head of the bed. "Welcome back." She flashed him a brilliant smile.

"Win." *What happened?*

"What did you say, Dr. Brady?"

"Win." *Why am I in the ICU? What happened?*

"Win. Win what? I don't understand."

He raised his head, looked directly at her, and spoke very slowly. "Win." *What happened to me? Why am I in the ICU?*

"I don't know what you mean by 'win.' I'm Lauren Levin. I'm your nurse."

"Win." *Quit playing games. I know who you are. Why am I here?*

"I'm sorry, Dr. Brady. I don't know what you mean by 'win.'"

He sighed and flopped back on his pillow. Why did she keep going on about win?

Lauren busied herself, taking his vital signs and adjusting the dressing around his left ear. He forced himself to relax and watched the well-known ICU routine—familiar, yet foreign from the viewpoint of a patient. Now everyone was taller than he was. Covered only by a single sheet and a flimsy gown bunched around his waist, he felt vulnerable and exposed—controlled, not in control.

She looked up when Mick Harrelson strode to the bedside. He had been on the staff for just over a year but already had a reputation as a brilliant neurosurgeon.

"Dr. Harrelson, he's awake. He seems to be alert, but I'm not sure how much he comprehends. He just keeps repeating the word 'win.' I don't know what that means."

Despite her turned back and hushed voice, Luke heard every word.

"Any other problems?" Mick asked.

"No. Neuro checks are normal. No drainage. No fever."

She glanced over her shoulder and grabbed his hand. "Dr. Brady, quit playing with your dressing; you'll pull out your drain."

Lauren retrieved a mirror from the bedside table and held it for him to see.

"Take a look," she said. "This is what you keep your hands off of."

His head was swathed in a thick gauze turban. A rubber drainage tube protruded from his left temple. He looked, made a combing motion with his left hand and raised his eyebrows.

She smiled. "Sorry, all gone. You're slicker than a cue ball."

She set the mirror on the table and stood aside.

Mick stepped to the bedside and laid his hand on Luke's shoulder. "Good morning, Luke. Glad you finally decided to rejoin us."

Luke reached his left hand toward Mick. "Win." *Mick, am I glad to see you. Maybe you'll tell me what the heck is going on.*

Mick grasped his hand. "Easy, Luke," he said. "Don't try to talk right now. You had an intracerebral bleed. I evacuated the clot, and everything looks stable. You've been unconscious for five days. Your right arm and leg are knocked out for now. You also have an expressive aphasia. No matter what you try to say, the only thing that comes out is 'win.'"

He paused, giving Luke time to digest this.

"Do you understand?"

"Win." *Of course I do. I've treated strokes before.*

Mick patted Luke's arm at the inevitable "win."

"Don't try to talk. It'll only frustrate you." Then with a smile, he added, "Not to mention me and everyone else. Can you move your head yes or no?"

Luke returned the smile and nodded yes.

"Good. Now do you understand what I've told you?"

Again he nodded yes.

"OK. You know this as well as I do. You're as bad as you're going to get. As the swelling goes down and compromised cells recover, with time and therapy, you will improve. How much is anyone's guess right now."

Luke nodded. Yeah, he understood. He'd given this same talk to scores of stroke patients. Many of them improved very little.

Mick turned to leave. "See you in the morning. We'll probably get you to a room tomorrow and start rehab in two to three days." He nodded toward the nurses' station. "Kate Minnick is here. You had several seizures early on, but she has them under control. Don't crack her up with any of your corny jokes," he said and chuckled.

Kate, the chief of neurology, finished studying the computer and strode toward his bed. She reminded Luke of a stumpy linebacker.

"He's awake and looking good," Mick said to her as she brushed past.

"Umm," Kate grunted without looking up.

"He hasn't had a seizure in three days," Lauren said.

"Umm," Kate replied. She checked Luke's reflexes. "Squeeze my fingers," she instructed. "Umm." With no further comment, she returned to the desk.

Luke looked at Lauren, raised his eyebrows, and smiled.

Lauren closed the curtains and stifled a laugh.

"What a cold fish. I'll bet her orgasms are three blinks of her eyes and a twitch of her nose."

When Luke's familiar laugh burst out, she began giggling. "Thank God you didn't stroke your sense of humor."

She was still tittering when she brought his breakfast.

Julie Vacarro woke with a start. Since receiving word of her father's stroke five days ago, she had encamped in the ICU waiting room. Her classes and basketball team at the high school would just have to wait. Luke needed her. She unfolded herself from the oversized reclining chair, stretched, yawned, and walked to the secretary's desk. She wore a rumpled T-shirt and jeans. Her blond hair was pulled back into a ponytail.

"Dr. Harrelson didn't want to wake you," the secretary said. "He said he'd see you later. Do want to see your father now?"

"Thank you. I'll wait for my mother."

"I'll notify the nurse when she arrives," the secretary said.

Julie threaded her way through a maze of other families' makeshift beds to the coffee urn. She stood sipping her coffee and gazing out the room's only window. Haze from Atlanta's late August heat and humidity had already started to blur the skyline. A shaft of early sunlight highlighted a night shift nurse trudging to her car. She slipped off her backpack, threw it into the back seat, and slid in. Others filtered into the parking lot. Julie had been outside twice since Luke was admitted. During the long hours of tedious waiting in the glimmer of artificial light, she remained oriented by her watch and frequent trips to the window. She jumped when the secretary touched her arm.

"Mrs. Vaccaro, your family's here."

Julie rushed to the two women standing by the door. "Aunt Mary, I'm so glad you could come," she said, throwing her arms around the taller one. "Will you be able to stay awhile?"

"Three or four days. Helen's letting me use your old bedroom."

"Good morning, Mother."

Helen Brady stiffened when Julie kissed her cheek. She did not return the kiss.

⟞⟊⟊⟝

Lauren met them outside the ICU entrance.

"Good morning," she said. "Have you spoken with Dr. Harrelson?"

"He left before I got here," Helen Brady said with obvious irritation. Her erect carriage, expensive dress, and neatly coifed hair conferred an air of elegance, which was offset by her cool manner and the hard set of her mouth. "The secretary said he didn't want to wake me up," Julie said. "I didn't doze off until after three. Those chairs were designed for something between sitting and lying down. Not real conducive to sleeping." Even without makeup, her large brown eyes and firm jaw were striking. It was obvious she was Luke's daughter.

"I told you to come home with me," Helen sniped.

9

Ignoring her, Julie turned to Lauren. "How's Daddy?" she asked.

"He's much better. No seizures. He's awake and moving his left side."

"That's wonderful," Julie said. Then, after a pause, she asked, "Is he…you know…with it?"

"Yes. He recognizes the doctors and me. He can follow simple commands. He laughs at my jokes."

Julie's worried expression eased.

"There are some problems," Lauren continued.

"What?"

"He has little motion on his right side. He can move his head yes or no, but he can't talk."

"Why?" Julie asked.

"Dr. Harrelson can explain better than I, but basically, the hemorrhage severely damaged the area of his brain that controls speech. Dr. Brady knows what he wants to say, but he can't get it out. He can only say one word, 'win.'" She looked at Julie. "Any idea what it means?"

Julie shook her head. "No, I can't think of anything."

Lauren turned to Helen.

"I haven't an inkling. Could we go in now? I have a nine o'clock appointment."

Lauren opened the door.

Julie gave an apologetic smile and followed her mother. Mary trailed close behind.

Before leading them to his bed, Lauren cautioned them, "He can't see anything to the right. He doesn't realize this yet. Stand on the left side, and he'll have no trouble seeing you."

Luke's smile lit up his face when he saw them. "Win." *I'm so glad you're here.*

Julie flinched when he spoke but grasped his hand and thrilled at his firm return squeeze. She kissed his hand and pressed it to her cheek, afraid to get near the bulky bandage with the rubber drain.

"Daddy, I've been so worried. How do you feel?"

"Win." *Pretty good, considering.*

Julie berated herself. "Are you OK?"

He nodded his head.

"Do you hurt?"

He smiled and waggled his hand.

She stepped back. "Mother, doesn't he look good?"

Helen stepped closer to the bedside but made no physical contact. "You do look better, Luke."

Luke smiled and laughed from time to time at Julie's animated chatter. Helen stood slightly to the side, shifting from foot to foot and saying little.

After fifteen minutes Lauren returned. "We need to get him cleaned up and fed. You can come back after lunch."

Julie kissed his hand once more. "I'll be just outside, Daddy."

"I'll try to come back later," Helen said, then turned and left.

Mary spoke briefly with him, squeezed his hand and kissed his cheek. "Hang in there, little brother."

Luke's gaze trailed them as they left. Julie stopped at the door, flashed him a smile, and blew him a kiss, both of which he returned. She turned, but not before he saw the tears streaming down her cheeks.

⚓⚓

"Will you be coming home tonight?" Helen asked, ignoring the tears.

Julie swiped her face with her bare hand. "It depends on how he does. Probably not."

Helen shrugged. "Let me know when you decide." She looked at her watch. "I must go," she said and left.

"Have you had breakfast?" Mary asked.

"No, and I'm starved," Julie said.

"Let's go to the diner across the street, I could use some coffee."

Mary followed Julie to a booth in the rear. Julie was every inch an athlete—slender, but solid from four years of collegiate basketball. She moved with a lithe grace, and at six feet, was two inches shorter than Luke. The smell of food perked her up but couldn't dispel her worried expression.

Mary nursed her coffee as Julie wolfed down scrambled eggs, bacon, and pancakes.

"Luke looks better than I thought he would," Mary said.

"I'm scared to death for him," Julie said. "He can practice from a wheelchair, but what if he's not able to talk? Daddy communicates so well with his patients and students. If he can't practice medicine and teach, I'm afraid he'll just give up."

"I've known Luke far longer than you. He's tough and resilient, always has been. He won't quit. He's a survivor," Mary said.

"I hope so. He'll need it. Mother's already talking about putting him in a nursing home," Julie said.

"This was so unexpected. She's still in shock."

"She means it," Julie said. "You saw her—cold, unemotional, just like always. Her only emotions I remember were anger, frustration, and impatience." Tears began streaming down her cheeks. "She almost never hugged or kissed me or even had a conversation with me except to tell me what I did wrong or what I should or shouldn't do."

Before Mary could speak, Julie blurted, "I wish you were my mother. I loved it when I came to your home in the summer."

Mary smiled and sipped the last of her coffee. "Don't be too harsh. Your mother wasn't always this way. Sometimes life just sucks you dry. She does the best she can."

"What do you mean?"

Mary shrugged. "Come on, let's go."

⊱─━┈━─⊰

Lauren fluffed Luke's pillow and straightened him in the bed.

"Mrs. Brady is beautiful—so elegant," she said.

Luke nodded. *You think she's pretty now. You should have seen her then.*

His mind drifted to the day in the library when he first saw her. Could it have been forty years? It seemed like yesterday...

He was hunkered down in a library carrel, plowing through the biochemistry of proteins and amino acids. This isolated corner in the medieval English literature section had been his private study hall since he found it his freshman year. The musty odor of mold and dust wafted around the dated volumes, through the stacks, down the aisles. Few ventured into this academic backwater. He had it all to himself.

He had little time for the usual college experience. If it weren't for his scholarship, a part-time job, and living at home, he would not have been able to attend at all.

His growling stomach reminded him he had skipped breakfast. He stood, stretched, and strode toward the back stairwell to get a soda. Rounding the end of the stack, he collided with a cart piled high with books. He toppled in a heap beneath an avalanche of tumbling texts that threatened to bury him.

"Oh, I'm so sorry. Are you hurt?" She bent over and lifted off several volumes.

Luke's eyes widened as he stared up at an image straight from the pages of *Vogue*. He leaned back and smiled up at her. "No. I've never been better."

She grabbed his hand and tugged. "Don't be silly. Come on. Get up."

He began handing her the scattered books. "Let me help you. It was my fault." They quickly stacked them in their proper order.

"Thank you," she said and turned to go.

He grasped the cart. "Miss...Miss...?"

"Winston. Helen Winston." Her smile lit up the aisle.

"Luke Brady." He hesitated. "Have you had lunch?"

She shook her head and lifted a brown sack from the bottom shelf of the cart.

"Mine's back at the carrel. Would you have lunch with me?"

Another breathtaking smile. "That sounds good."

They sat in the shade of an oak behind the library.

He couldn't stop looking at her. She was tall, with long flaxen hair and icy-blue eyes.

"Aren't you going to eat?" Helen asked.

He fumbled with the peel, then dropped his banana. Red-faced, he retrieved an apple from the plastic bag.

"What's your major?" Helen asked.

"Premed. Four more months and it's off to the big city and medical school."

"Your father a doctor?"

"No. He works here for the city utility department. I'm a live-at-home townie working my way through as a weekend lab tech. You?"

"Not much to tell. I'm a senior, too. Business major. My folks are farmers. Not too successful. I have a band scholarship. With my flute, my job at the library, and," she held up the remnants of her sandwich, "a lot of peanut butter, I'm getting by."

Lunch together became a daily event, followed in short order by Sunday church, nightly study sessions, and an occasional dinner at Smoking Bob's barbecue joint.

He was inexperienced and ill at ease with girls, but it was different with Helen. He could talk with her without effort. Even better, she seemed interested in what he had to say.

Walking to the car after the Sunday evening service six weeks later, he asked her, "Want to do something different?"

"What do you mean?"

"I'd like to show you something special."

"What?"

"It's a surprise."

"OK."

She was silent as he drove to the edge of town and turned onto a side road winding up a large hill.

"Are you abducting me?" she teased.

"Do you want to be abducted?"

"Maybe. Depends on the abductor."

The road ended at a tall chain-link fence lit by a mercury light. "This is it?" she asked.

"No." He got out, walked around the car, opened her door, helped her out, and pointed upward. "That."

A huge water tank loomed above them.

"I am surprised," she said. "What's so special about a municipal water tank?"

He unlocked the gate. "Nothing down here." He pointed and said, "Up there."

He took her hand and started walking toward the structure.

"You sure this is OK?" she asked.

"It's OK. I got the key from my dad. I've been here lots of times."

He stopped at the foot of the ladder.

"Do heights bother you?" he asked.

"You kidding?" She started up the ladder. "This isn't much taller than our silo back home." She paused about twenty feet up. "Are you coming, or are you just going to stand there gawking up my skirt?"

He laughed and began climbing.

He led her around the platform encircling the girth of the tank. Valdosta spread out below them. "There's the college. The library is just to the right." He pointed to other landmarks. They sat down on the backside of the tank. Shielded from the town lights, they gazed at the stars that sparkled above them, undimmed by the thin smile of a crescent moon.

"My grandmother said that kind of moon comes to gather the souls of those who have died," he said. "Each night for a month, it loads them in; then, when it's full, it transports them to heaven, lets them off, and starts over again."

"That's beautiful," she murmured.

"I've been coming here since I was twelve. It's where I come to unwind, to think, to dream."

"And what do you dream about?"

He paused. Sharing was not one of his strong points, but with Helen it was easier. "Being a doctor. A small-town doctor."

"That's all?" she asked.

"And having a big family."

"You're going to need some help on the last part."

He turned and took her hand. "Would you like to be a part of my dream?"

She smiled. "I think I might. I'll take it under advisement."

They were married right after graduation.

The years of medical school and residency passed quickly. They were poor but didn't realize it. Luke continued to work when he could. Helen's business acumen blossomed. She began as a receptionist in a clinic, but within two years was the office manager of a large group practice. She had also been the dynamo who energized and added sparkle to their marriage.

Luke smiled, remembering a day during his last year of medical school. When he arrived at their apartment, the strains of Helen's favorite flute concerto drifted from the back bedroom.

Helen sat on a stool by the window, swaying to the rhythm of the tune. She was completely naked.

Sensing his presence, she turned, stood, and smiled at his stunned expression.

"What?" she asked. "Can't a female flautist flaunt her figure for her fellow?"

He burst out laughing. "You shameless tease; you'd better watch out. You know alliteration acts as an aphrodisiac on me."

She laid the flute aside and threw the bedcovers down. "Prove it."

A commotion in the adjacent bed shattered his reverie. His face clouded as he tried to recapture the mood.

They had been so happy. Helen kept their home on an even keel. She remained funny and full of life. After his residency, she assumed the role of office manager and doctor's wife without complaint. She kept the stress level low at the office and at home, allowing him to concentrate on his medical practice.

Had it always been about him? His training. His practice. His patients. Had she noticed and resented it? Was that where it started? Was that why it proved so fragile?

CHAPTER THREE

Julie had just left. Luke looked at the pitiful remains of his lunch. He'd give anything for a steak, or even a salad—and a piece of key lime pie, he added as an afterthought.

He had been in the private room for three days. He had never realized how boring being a patient could be. After the early-morning rush of having blood drawn, being helped to bathe, and going to therapy, there was little to do until bedtime. Brief visits by Mike were a pleasant break in the monotony. The highlight of his days was mealtimes when Julie faithfully came to ensure he ate his bland pureed diet.

Luke had never been given to introspection. He largely ignored his inner life, devoting a majority of his quiet hours to reading medical journals or writing articles for other, smaller journals. Otherwise, either by choice or by temperament, he had to be active. He spent most of his time seeing patients, teaching, jogging, or visiting colleagues.

Now, he occupied himself plodding back and forth with his walker, trying to accelerate his physical therapy. Profound fatigue limited his exercise. He had always warned his stroke patients about this poststroke exhaustion, but he had no concept of how debilitating it was. He had to rest every ten or fifteen minutes. Even during his rest periods, he worked with his fumbling right hand: squeezing the rubber ball they gave him, sorting and stacking coins, playing the wooden peg game with golf tees. To heck with the fatigue; he was going to recover. A stroke wasn't going to undo twenty-five years of work. But he had to be able to talk. He could practice, teach, and even lead a medical school with a limp or a clumsy hand. But he had to be able to communicate.

Since he seldom watched TV and trying to read with his impaired vision gave him a splitting headache, he spent most of his spare time watching people in the park below his window. He could even see the bench under a large maple tree where he had often eaten lunch and fed the pigeons. This sufficed to keep his idle moments occupied.

The worst time was when Julie left after dinner. His diversions fled him. It was dark outside. He was too fatigued to walk or exercise and had little choice but to sit alone with his thoughts. Worries about the future and regrets about the past wrestled each other until he slipped into a fitful sleep.

Today after lunch there was a tap on his door, and Pamela Jackson, his nurse, entered. "Dr. Brady, I just got a call. Your doctor is bringing some students to see you on teaching rounds. They didn't ask, and I wanted to be sure you felt up to it."

Luke nodded eagerly. He tried to avoid talking since it seemed to upset everyone when he spoke.

From the time he came on the staff of the medical school, teaching rounds had been his favorite activity. Physical diagnosis was his forte. His book, *Basics of Physical Diagnosis,* had become the standard text at Macmillan and several other medical schools. He took pride in helping his students learn to show care and concern while conducting a thorough examination. For now, if he couldn't teach, maybe he could help them by being a voluntary guinea pig.

Without warning, the door burst open and Kate Minnick, followed by an entourage of two residents and five students, swept in.

Darn, he expected Mick.

Barely glancing at him, she stepped to the head of the bed and began to speak in a monotone, almost as if she were dictating.

"This is a sixty-two-year old male with a previously undetected cerebral aneurysm that ruptured, causing a massive intracerebral hemorrhage into the left hemisphere. Fortunately, this happened here in the medical center. The aneurysm was clipped and the clot evacuated within an hour. Despite this prompt intervention, Broca's speech area was destroyed, leaving him with a profound expressive aphasia."

Hey, Doctor, I'm here. Talk to me.

She ignored the angry "win" he sputtered and continued.

"He had several seizures the first forty-eight hours but none since. He has weakness of his right arm and leg. He also has a right homonymous hemianopia."

One student hesitantly raised his hand.

"Yes," she snapped.

"I'm not familiar with that term."

"He can't see anything to the right of the midline. I suggest you get familiar with that and any other terms relating to the patients assigned to you."

She then methodically conducted a complete neurological exam, demonstrating each deficit and loss.

"Open your mouth," she instructed, demonstrating by opening hers widely.

Gazing into her gaping maw, Luke almost laughed, but he complied.

She thrust the tongue blade against the back of his throat, causing him to gag and cough.

"As you see, he has a good gag reflex, so his swallowing should be adequate. He probably won't need a feeding tube."

No one moved or spoke.

"Doesn't anyone have any questions?" she asked.

"What do you do now?" a student asked.

"We've already started physical and occupational therapy. We'll begin speech therapy at the rehab center.

"What sort of response do you expect?"

"The visual impairment will likely clear as the edema subsides. The speech loss is almost certainly permanent," she said without hesitation. "He could possibly regain enough function on his right side to ambulate with a walker."

"How much does he comprehend?" a student at the rear asked an instant before being knocked breathless by an elbow in his ribs.

"Shut up, Snyder," the elbower muttered. "Damn."

"He seems to understand simple commands, but I doubt there is much more than that." She paused and glanced down at him. "It's a shame. He was a brilliant clinician."

He struggled to sit up and fixed her with a withering glare. "Win. Win. Win," he spat. *You arrogant, unfeeling clod. I'm still twice the clinician and ten times human being you are.*

To all but the most obtuse, he was violently angry.

Unperturbed, Kate Minnick walked to the door, pausing only to speak to Pamela. "The students appear to have upset him. He seems a bit agitated."

The elbower hung back after the others left. He walked to the bedside. "Dr. Brady, I'm Jim Nichols. I was in your bedside manners class. I'm so sorry. Snyder's an idiot. He and Dr. Minnick could both use that class."

Luke fought to regain control and gazed up at the sincere young man. With his good left hand, he grasped the student's arm and nodded. "Win." *Thank you, Doctor. Don't change.*

He lay back and took deep breaths. He might as well have been a mannequin or a cadaver. Except for Jim Nichols, everyone talked about him, but no one talked to him. The important thing was his stroke, not him. When he had calmed, he thought of the many times he had led similar groups of students and residents into patients' rooms unannounced. Had he focused on the disease and its signs and symptoms? Had he considered the impact of the disease on the patients, their jobs, their families, their futures? He hoped to heaven he'd done better than Kate Minnick.

The frightening thing was she might be right. He had seen a few similar stroke patients, some even worse, make remarkable recoveries. Most, however, improved little, if at all. He resolved if hard work had anything to do with it, then he would be one of the remarkable few.

━⟨⊹⊹⟩━

Outside his window, the sun was setting. A tap on the door jarred Luke from his melancholy ruminations. He gave Julie a wan smile when she entered. She kissed him on the cheek. "I know all about it. Forget her. She's forgettable."

Easy for you to say.

She pulled a chair to his bedside. "Could you use some good news?"

He rolled his eyes and nodded vigorously. *God, yes.*

"Good news number one: you're going to the university rehab center the first of next week. I took a tour after lunch. I was impressed. Are you familiar with it?"

He nodded.

"Dr. Harrelson said the staff journal club is planning to move their meetings there, so you can still be a part of it." She paused. "I know what you're thinking. He said you could have a beer with the others, but he would enforce a limit of two. Oh, and about your rehab, I'm going to keep close tabs on you. You'd better work hard, or I'll be all over you just like I am when my team underachieves. Understand?"

He smiled and nodded.

The rattle of dinner trays outside caused her to pause. She met the dietary aide, took the tray, and placed it on the bedside table. After getting him situated, she whipped off the cover, revealing a broiled chicken breast, mashed potatoes, and a bowl of strawberry gelatin. "Good news number two: real food, I think," she said, dubiously eyeing the tray. "Well, not pheasant under glass but better than pureed beets."

She cut up the meat and handed him the fork. "I know you're not left-handed, but do your best and take your time. Remember, anything that falls on the floor stays on the floor."

She chatted and ignored dropped food as he painstakingly lifted the food to his mouth. Despite his clumsiness, he had the plate clean in less than ten minutes. They both laughed when the squiggly gelatin leaped from his spoon and skittered around the tray while he tried to corner it. Finally, it too was gone.

"Last, but not least," she said and reached into her tote bag. "Ta-da, good news number three." A broad smile split his face as she whipped out a generous piece of key lime pie topped with whipped cream.

You're not only beautiful, but also a mind reader.

"I know it's not on your diet, but Dr. Harrelson said you deserved something for surviving. He also told me to destroy the evidence when you finished."

Minutes later he lay back, smiling contentedly while she discarded the empty Styrofoam container.

Pamela, his nurse, came and took the tray. "Good job," she said. Luke smiled and waved at her.

Julie pulled a chair to the bedside, sat, and took his hand. "Daddy, I saved the best news for last."

She hesitated.

Come on, come on. He motioned impatiently.

"I'm going to have a baby."

He smiled at her and uttered a hearty "Win." *Julie, I'm so happy for you.*

"I haven't told Mother yet. I'm sure she thinks we can't afford a child, but the timing is perfect. Mark's computer consulting business is picking up. It's not due until late May, so I'll be able to finish the school year and have two months before going back to work. We'll make out just fine."

She paused. "If it's a boy, we're going to name him Luke."

Luke choked up looking at her beaming face. He could only nod his head and smile.

━╫ ╫━

It was almost midnight before he could calm himself enough to drift off to sleep. He was standing by the fountain outside the main entrance to the hospital. A chartreuse grasshopper struggled to clamber out of the water. He stooped to rescue it. In an instant the huge fish with glowing eyes clamped on to his hand. His scream became a noisy gurgle as it yanked him under.

"Dr. Brady, are you OK?" the nurse asked.

His gaze darted around the room as he tried to orient himself.

She quickly checked his vital signs.

"Do you hurt anywhere?"

He shook his head.

"Are you sure you're OK?"

He nodded.

She watched him a few minutes more before she left. The sun was just rising when he dozed again.

Luke was eating breakfast when Mick Harrelson walked in and sat down. "Luke, you look great. The hair helps a lot."

Luke smiled. His hair had grown back and was cropped short as usual. He had hoped it would be darker, but despite positive thinking and psychic visualization, it remained gray.

"You've made fantastic progress in just three weeks," Mick said. Luke resumed eating. He could feel Mick's gaze as he painstakingly guided the fork in the general vicinity of his mouth. After several earlier jabs in the lip, he'd found it more efficient to hold the fork still and move his mouth forward to engulf it. He did better with his bumbling left hand, but he insisted on using his stroke-damaged right. He could control his head better than either. The spattered drops of food on his disposable bib indicated he still had a way to go.

Mick chatted idly and updated him on the latest hospital gossip. He glanced at his watch and stood. "Have to run. Got a case in twenty minutes." He laid his hand on Luke's shoulder. "Keep hard at it. The medical school needs your leadership. The students need your example."

Luke smiled and gave him a thumbs-up.

Mick was right. He had improved a lot. The therapists pushed him, but he pushed himself even harder. He charged into his morning sessions with enthusiasm.

Physical therapy from nine to ten thirty. He could now walk between the parallel bars without using the rails for balance. His gait was slow but steady. His right leg still had a tendency to drag, and his right foot slapped unless he placed it consciously. He felt he could get about with nothing but a cane, but the therapist insisted he use a walker.

Occupational therapy, eleven to noon, went a little slower. He gave a rueful smile, remembering his food-soiled bib. The strength in his right hand was nearly normal, but his fine motor function lagged. He could shower himself. Shaving was hazardous. After using two squares of toilet paper to stanch the oozing from nicks, he opted for an electric razor. Dressing himself was no problem, but manipulating buttons was slow and laborious.

Speech therapy, one thirty to three, was a nightmare. Yesterday was typical.

Sherry, the therapist, pointed to a picture of a beetle. "This is a bug," she said.

"Win." *Bug.*

"No. Not win. Bug. Make a B sound…Buh."

"Buh."

"Good, now an U…Uh."

"Uh."

"And now a G…Guh."

"Guh."

"Now put them together. Buh-uh-guh. Bug."

"Win." *Bug.*

Sherry sighed at the predictable "win." "Try it again. Buh-uh-guh."

"Win." *Bug.*

"Let's try this," she said and placed a digital recorder on the table before him. She clicked it on. "Now try it again. Buh-uh-guh."

Luke concentrated, willing the syllables to come. "Win." *Bug.*

"Listen." She clicked the recorder on.

Luke listened intently as Sherry's recorded voice spoke. "Now try it again. Buh-uh-guh."

Luke clenched his jaw when he heard his voice. "Win."

He heard "win" on the tape, but he heard "bug" in his head.

That evening he retrieved the Gideon Bible from the bedside table. He turned to Psalms and began reading, *The Lord is my shepherd, I shall not want...*He repeated, reading the Psalm aloud for three hours until he could finish it without a single hitch.

After lunch the next day, he put the Bible in the basket on his walker and plodded to speech therapy.

Sherry was arranging syllabic flash cards when he entered the room. He pushed them aside and motioned Sherry to sit down. He opened the Bible, pulled the recorder before him, and clicked it on. He spoke into the mic with a firm voice. *The Lord is my shepherd...*He read the entire psalm and concluded confidently...*and I will dwell in the house of the Lord forever.*

He pressed Back, gave Sherry a reassuring smile, and punched Play.

His playback voice didn't waver. "Win...win...win..." He slumped into his chair. Tears brimmed in his eyes.

Sherry put her arm around his shoulder. "Dr. Brady, I'm so sorry. Please don't give up."

Luke shrugged off her arm, stood, and picked up the Bible. He studied it for a moment, then hurled it across the room. Without looking back, he clumped out.

After brooding all afternoon and into the night, Luke plowed back into his therapy with renewed vigor. After his scheduled sessions, he spent the afternoons walking the halls or doing deep knee bends and push-ups in his room. To better control his stroke-impaired right hand, he stacked and unstacked coins. He tried unsuccessfully to shuffle cards but dealt them and played solitaire with increasing facility. He willed himself to spend an hour writing each day. This exasperated him because he could transmit thoughts through his hand to the paper no better than to his mouth and vocal cords. If the neural pathways from ideation to pen to paper could somehow be recovered more quickly than his injured speech channels, he wanted to be physically prepared. Like a ninth-century monk hunched in his cell, reproducing sacred writ, he copied articles from any printed material he could find. His writing progressed glacially from indecipherable glyphs to shaky block letters.

He knew, however, if he were ever to teach again, he must regain his speech. His achievements as a doctor depended on his relational skills. The students had voted him the best teacher on the staff more times than any other instructor. He was known as a superb diagnostician. Some of his diagnostic skill was because of his meticulous physical examinations; much resulted from his ability to communicate with patients. He was a master of setting a patient at ease and teasing out subtle symptoms that steered him to the correct diagnosis. This required speaking. He had to talk.

He tried every exercise the speech therapist suggested. When he was alone, he read aloud articles from newspapers, magazines, and medical journals. He read until he was hoarse. He never heard "win" when he spoke, only the intended words. But at each session, the hateful recorder crushed his dogged efforts with a litany of win...win...win. After each setback, like Sisyphus and his rock, he stubbornly began again.

The medical director and social worker sat across the table from Helen and Luke.

"Mrs. Brady, this is Dr. Brady's sixty-day evaluation meeting." He glanced at the chart. "Dr. Brady, you've made remarkable progress in physical and occupational therapy—not so much in speech therapy." He studied the chart and continued without looking up.

"You have improved to the point where you no longer qualify for comprehensive skilled care."

"What does that mean?" Helen asked.

"Your insurance will cover only intermediate care."

"So..." Helen said.

"Dr. Brady will be receiving therapy and care as before, but your insurance will not cover the full cost of such ongoing treatment. I'm sure Dr. Brady understands."

Luke smiled and nodded. He had given this same speech many times. No problem, though. He had good long-term care insurance.

"How much will not be covered?" Helen asked with an edge to her voice.

"Approximately two thousand dollars a month."

"That's out of the question," Helen snapped. "I've checked around. Our insurance more than covers the full costs at several nursing homes. There's a very nice one where he used to practice."

"I understand," the director said, "but no one else in the Southeast has the staff and facilities we have. Dr. Harrelson has even gotten Dr. Brady enrolled in a very promising experimental speech therapy program."

"We just can't afford it," Helen said.

Luke felt his stomach turn. *Helen, what are you thinking? This is the only chance I have of getting my speech back. We have the money.*

The director closed the chart and stood. "Please think it over. Let us work with him, if only for another month or two."

"When do you need an answer?" Helen asked.

"Within a week."

"Mother, you can't put Daddy in that nursing home," Julie protested.

"And what do you expect me to do, Julie?" Helen snapped. "They say his insurance won't cover this level of care any longer."

"But just for a month or two," Julie protested.

"I told you. We don't have the money."

"Couldn't he come home? He's getting around pretty well with a walker. We could get home physical and speech therapy. That would be cheaper than a nursing home. I could come on weekends, and I'm sure Aunt Mary will help out."

"I can't stay at home nursing him. Since his stroke, how many times has Mary been to see him? Two? Three? You can't quit your job. I'm the one who'll be tied down."

"But you're his wife."

"We live in the same house. He left me years ago."

"He'd do it for you."

Helen clenched her jaw. "I'm sure he would. His exaggerated sense of duty would compel him to."

"That's not fair, Mother."

"He's not the saint you think he is," Helen said.

"What do you mean?"

"Just forget it. This is the way it's going to be."

"At least put him in one closer to the medical school. His friends and students could come visit him."

"Julie, I've told you, they all cost fifteen hundred to two thousand dollars a month more than his long-term care insurance will cover. I've got to think of myself."

"But Shadydale is understaffed and smells. It's way out in Buxton, an hour's drive from here. How will you see him?"

"He practiced there before coming to teach at the medical school. I'm sure there are some old friends around. I'll see him when I can."

"That was twenty-five years ago—before I was born. How many friends are left?"

"The matter's settled. I don't want to talk about it anymore." She looked at her watch. "I'm late for my meeting."

With no further word, she threw on her coat and left.

CHAPTER FOUR

Jimmy Jenkins stretched and checked the clock on the bedside table: 5:06 a.m. He had always been an early riser. This was his favorite time of day. Exploring time. Sometimes to the kitchen where they gave him a cup of coffee and an early sample of breakfast. Tuesdays (pancakes) and Thursdays (french toast) were his favorites. Sometimes he sneaked through the door in the trash room, the only unalarmed door in the building, into the central courtyard to listen to the birds and watch the sun rise. Usually, he detoured to the lobby to see if the morning papers had been slipped through the slot in the door. He liked to read the comics and local sports in the community paper before the pages got crumpled; he saved his personal copy of the *Wall Street Journal* for later. Sometimes he prowled in other places.

The only sound this morning was the familiar squeak of Miss Benson's crepe-soled shoes as she made her early morning rounds. Her full name was Martha Q. Benson. No one knew what the Q stood for. To Jimmy, she was queen bee, but never to her face. She said she came in two hours early to be sure everything was in order for the main shift at seven. But Jimmy knew better. Jimmy knew just about everything that went on at Shadydale nursing home.

This morning, he would just go to the main nurses' station. A new night supervisor was supposed to have started last evening, and he wanted to check her out before shift change.

He tiptoed to the bathroom, taking care not to let the latch click when he shut the door. Pops liked to sleep as late as possible. He hung his pajamas on the back of the door, then peed. He didn't flush. That always woke Pops. Quietly, Jimmy wrestled with his briefs, jeans, and T-shirt. Dressing was a real chore.

Sitting on the toilet, he yanked on his socks and tugged on his shoes, taking care to fasten the Velcro tabs tightly. He ached for some signature high-top basketball shoes, but their long laces were just too much for his spastic fingers to handle.

He slipped the door open and padded toward the hallway. It was so quiet. Pops usually snored, or at least breathed through his nose with a loud whistle.

He edged toward Pops's bed. Pops lay flat on his back, silent. The covers didn't move.

"Pops, you awake?" No answer. He grasped his arm and shook it. "Come on, Pops, wake up." No response.

He clicked on the lamp and bent to look. Pops's wide, blank eyes were fixed on the ceiling.

"Aah! Aah!" Jimmy stumbled back from the bed and crashed to the floor, upsetting a small table and scattering chess pieces across the room. He scrambled to his feet and banged his shoulder on the doorframe as he floundered into the hall. Running only made him clumsier, but he had to get away from that room and get help for Pops. His right foot snagged his left heel, and he flopped into a tangled heap. He clawed at the handrail, dragged himself up, and blundered on, falling for the third time three feet from the nurses' station.

"What's the matter? Are you hurt?" Amy Maxwell, the new nurse, rushed to help him up.

"It's Pops. You've got to help Pops," he stammered.

Rounding the corner, Martha Benson rushed up. "What's going on here, Amy?" She ignored Jimmy, who lay crying on the floor.

"I don't know. Something about 'Pops,'" Amy said.

Miss Benson pointed to two nursing assistants. "You take care of this idiot." Then, already on the move, she said to the other CNA and Amy, "Room one twenty-five; come with me."

She shook Pops and felt his cold neck for a pulse.

"Help me get him on the floor. I'll start CPR, and you call nine-one-one."

Amy hesitated. "He's dead."

Martha tugged his legs off the bed. "I told you to help me get him onto the floor and call nine-one-one," she screamed.

Amy helped turn him onto his back, then dialed the bedside phone. The call completed, she knelt to help Martha, who was pumping on Pops's rigid chest. They rose and stepped back when the EMTs charged into the room.

Jack, the head EMT, conducted a rapid survey.

"Damn, Nurse Benson, he's stiff. What were you thinking?"

"He didn't have DNR instructions. I told him a hundred times to get it done, but he refused. Protocol says if there are no DNR instructions, we're to do CPR until the EMTs arrive. You do your job. I'll do mine."

Jack shrugged. "Well, we're here, and I say he's dead." He turned to his partner. "Help me get him on the gurney, and let's get out of here."

Martha glared at them until they left. Still red-faced and perspiring, she brushed stray strands of her bright-red hair from her face. "Don't just stand there gawking. The morning shift will be here in an hour." She snapped her fingers at the nursing assistant. "Get this cleaned up."

Halfway to the nurses' station, she told Amy, "Come to my office in fifteen minutes." Then, shoes squeaking, she strode off.

⚒

"Is she always like this?" Amy asked Joyce, the LPN.

"No," she answered. "This was a worst-case scenario. Miss Benson wants things to run smoothly at all times. She comes in two hours early to make sure they do. She's tough, but she's a very good nurse. It just upsets her when things get out of control."

"What about him?" She nodded toward Jimmy. He had stopped crying, and the CNA was talking quietly to him.

"That's Jimmy. He's been here fourteen years."

"He looks awfully young to be in a nursing home."

"He's in his early thirties. He was born with severe cerebral palsy. His father divorced his mother and abandoned them a short time later. Fortunately, his mother's family was well-to-do. When she discovered she was dying from breast cancer, she set up a trust to pay for his care for the rest of his life. I've heard he's really wealthy. This is the only home he's known since she died."

"Is he usually this, you know, excitable?"

"Oh no, he's really sweet. He likes to help everybody—the staff, the patients, even the visitors. He was very close to Pops...Mr. Morrisey. They had been roommates for almost three years."

Amy busied herself, finishing the night's charting.

"You'd better get on down to Miss Benson's office," Joyce said.

Amy tapped on the door.

"Come in," Martha said.

Amy hesitated a moment and then opened the door.

Martha stood as she entered. Her makeup was again perfect, and every hair was in place. No hint of her previous agitation.

"Come in, Amy." She motioned to the chair. "Make yourself comfortable. Would you like some coffee?"

"No, thank you. I'm keyed up enough already."

"I understand. Some cold water?"

"That, I could use," Amy said.

Martha retrieved a bottle of water from a small fridge beneath her desk.

Amy took a long drink. "Miss Benson, I'm sorry about—"

"Don't let it bother you. You did just fine." She smiled and winked. "And please call me Martha." She sipped her coffee. "Don't worry about Jimmy. He's spastic but harmless."

Unsure if she was supposed to reply, Amy drank her water.

"I just want to be sure you're OK. Just your second day. That's a lot to handle."

"I've seen worse," Amy said.

They chatted amiably for ten more minutes.

"I need to get back to the floor," Martha said. "I want you to know how pleased we are to have you here. Good nurses are hard to find."

"I'm happy to be here."

"Well, if you ever need anything, my door is always open."

<hr />

Dr. Martin Luther Brown glanced at his watch: 10:25. "Damn." The two new admissions at the hospital had thrown him way behind. Despite the cold outside, a thin sheen of perspiration glistened on his ebony forehead. *They always keep it too warm in here.*

"What do we have this morning?" he asked Betty Johnson, the charge nurse.

"Slow down, Dr. Brown, relax. You did most of the recertifications Friday. No new patients and only five recerts today, two here and three on Wing Three. Mrs. Wilson has the sniffles, and Mr. Timmons is a little short of breath."

Betty understood the doctor must recertify patients' needs for continuing care each month in order for Medicare and Medicaid to pay for further treatment.

"Thank goodness. I might make the staff meeting at noon."

"Oh," Betty said, "Mr. Morrisey died this morning."

"Pops? That's too bad. How's Jimmy?"

"I haven't seen him today."

Martin nodded. Followed by the LPN pushing the chart rack, he walked to Wing One to begin rounds.

"Dr. Brown…"

He looked up from the last chart on Wing Three. Debbie Watson, the CNA, handed him a cup of hot coffee.

"Thank you, Debbie. I need that."

"Have you seen Jimmy yet?"

"No, how is he?"

"He's really upset. He loved Pops." Her eyes misted. "Could you talk with him?"

He looked at his watch and hesitated. "Yeah, do you know where he is?"

"He's out in the courtyard."

As he rose to leave, she touched his arm. "Thank you, Dr. Brown."

Protected by his puffy fleece coat, Jimmy sat huddled on the bench beneath the bare, leafless maple tree. Despite being doused by the bright morning sun and shielded on three sides by the building, the November air in the courtyard still bit with a wintry nip.

The gravel crunched beneath Martin's feet. Jimmy looked up and brushed at a stray tear from his cheek. Martin sat down and draped his arm around his shoulder.

"I'm so sorry about Pops."

"He was my best friend."

It had taken time, but by now Martin had no trouble understanding Jimmy's loud, high-pitched nasal voice, though today emotion made it even jerkier than usual.

"Yeah. He told me the other day how much he enjoyed playing chess with you."

Jimmy gave a crooked smile. "I let him win."

"I know...but he didn't."

Jimmy's smile broadened, then clouded. "What happened? He didn't feel bad at all last night. Then he was just lying there...staring." He started to tear up. "I sneaked him some ice cream before bedtime. That didn't hurt him, did it?"

"That had nothing at all to do with it. He was eighty years old and had had several heart attacks. Sometimes the heart just wears out and stops. He told me many times he never wanted to go back to the hospital. I think he would have wanted to go quickly with his best friend nearby."

Jimmy sat up straighter. "One time he told me, when his time came, he didn't want to hang around. He just wanted to kick the bucket and get it over with." He gave a brief laugh.

Martin stood and drank the last of his coffee. "It makes us sad, but we can take some comfort that he got his wish. And you know what, I think he'd want us to laugh, not cry, when we remember him."

"I think so, too."

⟞⟝

"Sorry I'm late."

It was like every other staff meeting since he had been medical director at Shadydale. The remains of two large deluxe pizzas

38

occupied the center of the long conference table. Dan Crandell, the portly administrator, sat at one end, a plate with three slices and the crusts of two more in front of him. His dark-brown hair was combed over in a vain attempt to hide his balding pate. His eyes were fixed on Martha Benson.

She was tall and statuesque. Her tight sweater emphasized her large breasts, the objects of Crandell's gaze. Her bright-red hair was pulled into a bun.

"I'm glad you could make it, Dr. Brown," she said with a hint of sarcasm. "We've just about finished the reports. Wilma, what's our current census?"

Wilma was the social services director. In fact, Wilma was the entire social services department and served as the secretary for staff meetings. She was a middle-aged, matronly woman who spoke with a regional twang.

"We have one hundred eighty-eight total patients, one hundred ten custodial care, twenty-eight dementias, and fifty skilled rehabs. I don't have the breakdown of the other skilled patients."

"We have a total of sixty-eight, including twelve tubers," Martha said. She gave a small smile when Martin winced at her description of patients receiving tube feedings. He had asked her several times not to use that term.

"Any new admissions this week, Wilma?"

"Two tomorrow and one Thursday, a doctor."

"A doctor—what's wrong with him?" Martha asked.

"Don't know," Wilma said. "They're faxing his records later today."

The meeting wound down as Crandell lifted the last slice of pizza from the box.

"I'd like to mention one thing for the medical director's report," Martin said.

"What is it?"

"I'm really concerned about the mattresses and plastic covers. They're all over five years old and sag. The covers are getting stiff and cracked. We're going to have more bedsores if they're not replaced."

"Don't record that," Crandell snapped at Wilma, who had started to scribble in her notes. "We'll discuss this later. I think that about winds things up. You can go ahead and start transcribing the minutes, Wilma."

Wilma gathered her notes and left.

"What was that about?" Crandell asked Martin.

"It's a real problem. If it's in the minutes where the inspectors can see it, corporate headquarters will have to do something about it."

"They are doing something."

"Two new mattresses and covers a month," Martin said. "At this rate it will take one hundred months to replace them all. Eight years."

"How's your practice doing, Dr. Brown? Paying well?" he asked.

"It's OK. Why?"

"You and I both know your director's stipend, the Medicare and Medicaid billings from our patients, are what's keeping you afloat."

"It helps," Martin said.

"Then why put it at risk over a few mattresses?"

Martin started to reply, then looked away, shook his head, and left.

><+ +>

Crandell headed for the door.

"Hold up a minute, Dan," Martha said and shut the door.

"What is it? Dr. Brown?"

"No, not that. He knows he can't do without us."

"What then?"

"I'm not sure about accepting a doctor for a patient. Doctors and their families are always dissatisfied, demanding, and a pain in the butt. I think we ought to skip this one."

"Not take him as a patient—are you crazy?"

"I'm just saying he could be more trouble than he's worth."

"He has private insurance. That's two thousand dollars a month more than we get from anybody else. If we had a hundred of those, then we wouldn't have to scrimp. We might not have to have a black medical director, a hick in social services, and a housekeeping service that's eighty percent undocumented. You and I could even get a raise. I'd say that's worth a bit of bother."

"I just feel uncomfortable about it."

"Get this straight. You tend to medical matters, and I'll take care of the finances."

"I don't know…"

"Look, he's from this area. He practiced in Buxton several years ago."

"What's his name?"

"Bradley, Broady. Something like that."

"Brady? Luke Brady?" Martha asked.

"Yeah, that's it. What difference does it make?"

Martha smiled. "None. None at all. Forget I said anything. It'll be just fine."

Martha closed the door to her office. She surveyed the plaques on the wall behind her desk. Martha Q. Benson, president, smiled back from her nursing school graduation picture. Surrounding this were her diploma from Macmillan College of Nursing, her master's certificate, two Macmillan Medical Center Nurse of the Year awards, and a certificate from the National Nursing Association

Honor Society. Her jaw clenched. *You were…you are a damned good nurse.* She spun around and sat at her desk, grabbed a tissue, and blew her nose. A smile crept across her face.

"Dr. Luke Brady. My, my, my."

She hummed a tune as she selected a key from the cluster in her pocket and unlocked the large lower drawer of her desk.

CHAPTER FIVE

Luke lay back, eyes closed, and squeezed the rubber ball in his right hand in time with the rhythms of *The Nutcracker*. Thanksgiving hadn't arrived, and they were already playing Christmas music. Even the music of the season couldn't lighten his foul mood. Didn't he have any say in what happened to him? He gave a derisive snort. *No, dummy, you have to be able to* say *to have a say*.

He heaved the ball against the wall and pounded his spastic hand on the serving table, bellowing threats and curses. *Damn you, Helen! You've finally won.*

His nurse rushed in. "Dr. Brady, Dr. Brady, calm down. Stop yelling 'win.' You're disturbing the other patients." She moved the table and lowered the head of his bed. "Why don't you take a nap. Your daughter will be here soon."

That's great, Luke. People can't even understand your cussing. Finally, he calmed and lay back.

He and Helen had lived in a state of undeclared war for twenty-five years. Both went their separate ways. They lived in the same house but slept in separate beds in separate rooms. Their one half-hearted effort at counseling came to nothing. The counselor had said Helen needed to work on forgiveness and he on making amends. Helen never tried. Forgiveness was not in her. She hurt him at every opportunity. To his credit, Luke made a sincere effort to atone for hurting her, but his very presence seemed to add to her pain.

Why had they stayed together? Julie, in large part. Perhaps Helen needed someone to hurt. In some twisted, masochistic logic, maybe he needed to be hurt and made to feel guilty. Over the years, hurts layered upon hurts, like barnacles on a ship too long at anchor.

But just as nature tends toward entropy, in time their conflict became less fierce, and they coexisted in an uneasy, painful détente.

The knock on his door brought him upright. He forced a flimsy smile when Julie and Mark entered, pushing a wheelchair.

"We didn't want you to have to go in an ambulance, so we're your limousine service," Julie said. She looked him over. "I'm glad you're dressed, and I must say, you look very dapper." She laid a large suitcase on the bed and began packing his clothes. "We have the last three months of *New England Journal* and *JAMA* in the car." She retrieved the ball, threw it on his clothes, and zipped the suitcase. "That does it," she said after a final survey of the room. "Time to hit the road."

Mark started forward with the wheelchair. Luke waved him back. He pulled the walker from the side of his chair, grasped the handles, and stood. Slowly he walked to the wheelchair and sat down.

"That was great, Dad," Mark said. "A little more work, and you'll be ready to take Julie dancing."

He didn't smile.

"There's the turnoff to Buxton. We'll be there in about ten minutes." Julie's voice yanked Luke from his nap. Feigning interest, he rubbed his eyes and stared out the window. Once upon a time, this had been a place of dreams, a place where he and Helen had established their safe haven, their future. Now the dreams were dead, the haven unsafe, and the future gone.

A lot had changed in twenty-five years. Scattered small houses and double-wides sat haphazardly in what had been nearly endless soybean fields. The hosiery mill stood bleak and shuttered. Its once bustling parking lot now hosted a huge flea market filled with ramshackle sheds and tents. Like the mill, he was a mere shell of that once optimistic young physician ready to take on the world.

Welcome home, Luke. His mood spiraled further downward. Why did Helen stick him out here in the boonies in a crummy nursing home in a backward place he never wanted to see again? He'd be getting cutting-edge therapy at university rehab. The research project Mick had enrolled him in might have really helped his speech. He could even meet with the guys at breakfast once or twice a week.

Screw you, Helen. He knew she had always worried about money, but this was ridiculous. His disability income plus the long-term care insurance and what he wouldn't be spending on professional expenses would easily cover everything with some left over. This was pure spite. He had spent twenty-five years trying to make it up to her. That should count for something.

"Here we are," Julie announced, cutting short his black ruminations.

Shadydale Recovery Center. The stucco-and-brick sign was unchanged save for some seasonal decorations: corn shocks, pumpkins, and gourds. The sprawling one-story brick building had been painted white. Three venerable oak trees, twenty-five years larger than before he left, gave evidence to its name.

Debbie met them at the door, helped him into a wheelchair, and pushed him to the main office.

Dan Crandell stepped from behind his desk. "Dr. Brady, welcome back to Shadydale." Luke made no move to clasp his outstretched hand. "This is Martha Benson, our director of nursing."

She gave him a tight smile, then turned to Julie. "Dr. Brown will see him in the morning. He says they were acquainted. Dr. Brady will start physical therapy Monday. I'm not sure how much longer we can keep him classified as skilled care."

"What does that mean?" Julie asked.

"It means when he is no longer making significant progress, his insurance will not pay for more therapy."

"I'm sure we can afford more if he needs it. We want him to—"

Martha cut Julie off. "That's your choice. All our private rooms are taken. He'll be in the room with Jimmy Jenkins. Jimmy's a little slow, but he's very friendly. I'm sure they'll get along fine."

"Win," Luke snapped. *Hey, lady, I'm right here. Talk to me.*

"I beg your pardon."

Julie grasped his hand. "Daddy has trouble with his speech. 'Win' is the only word he can say, but he can nod yes or no. Maybe your speech therapist can help."

"Maybe," Martha replied. "Can he understand anything of what's said to him?"

"Oh yes," Julie said. "That's no problem."

"Win," *Can you understand this?* Red-faced, Luke suppressed the urge to reply with the middle finger of his good left hand.

Martha chucked his cheek and winked. "We'll do just fine."

"Win." *I can hardly wait.*

⊷⊶

Luke sat on the edge of the bed and surveyed the room. As with the exterior, little inside was changed since he made rounds here so long ago. The furnishings were Spartan but functional. Two single hospital beds, each flanked by a reclining chair with a floor lamp and a side table with a straight-backed chair. Atop each table sat a lamp, a digital clock, and a Gideon Bible. To his right were the toilet and shower; on his left, by the door to the hallway, was a tall table with a TV and a smaller table on which sat a chess board with pieces placed ready for action. A large trunk stood at the foot of the other bed.

The mattress cover crackled as he flopped back on the bed and stared at the ceiling. He'd intended to walk around and refamiliarize himself with Shadydale, but despite three months of intense physical therapy, fatigue still overcame him at times during the day. Exhausted, he closed his eyes and began to drift. Then he slept.

⊷⊶

Through the window by the bed, the afternoon sun struck him squarely in the face. Shielding his eyes, he struggled to a sitting position. He yawned, stretched, and tried to orient himself.

He gave a start when his gaze fell on a young man hunched on the other bed, staring at him.

"Are you awake?" His high-pitched, nasal voice was halting and louder than need be.

Luke nodded.

His visitor clomped across the room and stretched out his hand. Their hands missed on the first try, then locked in a spastic handshake.

Luke sighed. *This is rich. Herky meets jerky.* He had been yanked away from his professional friends, dumped in the boonies, and now he was bunking with an obvious simpleton.

"I'm Jimmy Jenkins."

Right now, Luke didn't care who he was. He just wanted to be left alone.

"I'm your roommate."

Luke made no move to communicate.

"They'll be serving dinner in a few minutes. Are you hungry?"

Luke shook his head and looked around in desperation. *Go away.* He grabbed his walker, struggled to his feet, stumbled to the toilet, and shut the door. He remained there until he heard Jimmy leave the room.

Was there nowhere he could get some privacy? He needed to think, to have some time alone. He needed…hell, he didn't know what he needed.

He wasn't at all sure he could tolerate any roommate, particularly Jimmy Jenkins. He had not shared a room since Helen's departure to another bedroom after their relocation from Buxton to Atlanta twenty-five years ago. He was used to, and jealous of, his own personal, private space. He'd had private accommodations at university rehab. Was he rooming with Jimmy because there were no private rooms available at Shadydale, or because of Helen's penny-pinching?

Luke grabbed his walker and clattered from the room. With most residents in the dining room, the halls were nearly vacant.

Shadydale was laid out in the form of the letter H. The crossbar was elongated relative to the legs of the H and extended through them, leaving three patient wings on each end. A large nurses' station stood at the intersection of each set of patient wings. All of the administrative and working areas were clustered along the central hallway.

As he approached the nurses' station, a young woman in brown scrubs stepped forward. He recognized her as the one who had wheeled him into the building.

She pointed to her name tag. "Dr. Brady, I'm Debbie Watson. Do you need anything?"

He shook his head and moved to continue.

"Can I show you around?"

He glowered, shook his head, and plopped his walker forward.

Debbie flashed a radiant smile. "Well, if you need anything, just holler."

Slamming his walker down, he glared at her. "Win," he snapped. *If I could holler, I wouldn't be here, you little twit.*

She flushed. "Oh, I'm so sorry. They told me you couldn't speak." She laid her hand on his arm. "Please forgive me."

Still glaring, he jerked his arm away and rattled down the hall, leaving her red-faced.

"Move it, old timer," a gravelly voice demanded from behind.

A wizened, bushy-haired woman hunched in a wheelchair, propelling herself by rapidly shuffling her slippered feet, cruised past and left him in her wake.

He remembered nurses referring to this mode of locomotion as boogieing. He watched as she boogied down the hall and disappeared into a room on the left. Despite his foul mood, he chuckled. Some things never change.

He continued until he reached the lobby, then turned and plodded slowly back toward his room. As he approached the nurses' station, Debbie paused from straightening a patient in his chair. He caught her stricken look as she took a hesitant step toward him. Averting his gaze, he spun around and rushed back the way he had come.

When he passed the activities room, the bushy-haired lady was ensconced firmly in front of a TV set. *Must have been late for her soap.* Several others sat beside her. Two women bent over a jigsaw puzzle. Nothing had changed. They were no different from the lonely people sequestered here for the duration of their lives twenty-five years ago. How long before he would be content to watch TV, work jigsaw puzzles, solve find-a-word, or simply stare off into space?

Just past the activities room was a door labeled Chapel. When he had been here before, this had been two rooms: the social worker's office and a "quiet room" used to inform families of a loved one's worsening condition or death. Maybe he could have some privacy here. His walker rattled as he clambered through the door. The chapel was lit by several skylights, a small spotlight in the front, and what light filtered from the hallway through the small stained-glass window in the door. A center aisle separated six rows of short pews. He walked to the spotlit table in the front on which sat a cross and a King James Bible. Luke gave a rueful smile. Since there were precious few Jews and no Muslims in this part of Georgia, this must be deemed sufficient. He needed a place like this. It was nice. It was quiet and peaceful. It was deserted.

Not bothering to turn on the lights, he sat on a pew in the rear, leaned back, closed his eyes, and took long, deep breaths, willing himself to relax. What was the matter with him? Wallowing in self-pity? Two sweet young people have tried to be nice, and he blew them off. How many more people would he hurt? This wasn't him. But dammit, he wasn't him.

After several minutes, his agitation eased. *Come on, Luke. Get ahold on yourself. How many people have you sent to this very facility? You're stuck here. Make the best of it. And clean up your language.* He had cursed more in the past week than he could remember. He was just so angry—at his situation, at Helen, at God, at anything that moved.

He sat in quiet contemplation for the next three hours. His anger slowly receded. He was nearing his usual easygoing disposition when he returned to his room. To his relief, Jimmy wasn't there. On his bedside table stood a bottle of water, a sandwich, and a cold piece of apple pie. *Luke Brady, you are a first-class jerk.* Despite his self-assessment, he ate it all.

He pretended to be asleep when Jimmy returned and did the same the next morning. The dining room was almost empty when he reached a table in the far corner.

He was just finishing his oatmeal and toast when Miss Benson strode in.

"Debbie, go get Brady and take him to the examining room to see Dr. Brown," she snapped in a loud voice.

"Dr. Brady?" Debbie said.

"Yes, *Dr.* Brady. No big deal. He's no different from all the other strokes."

Debbie started for his table.

"Take the wheelchair. We don't have time for him to hobble there."

Luke winced and muttered, "Win." *I'd like to hobble you.* He suppressed adding an expletive.

"Dr. Brady, I'm so sorry about yesterday."

He patted her hand and nodded.

"Are you through with breakfast?"

He wore the standard nursing home uniform: gray sweatshirt and pants with elastic around the waistband and ankles—codger pants, he called them. He had balked at the cloth, rubber-soled slippers and wore his own shoes. Bits of food lay scattered around his plate and dribbled down the front of his shirt. He smiled and nodded again.

She wiped some crumbs from the corner of his mouth and his shirt.

"There. Ready to go?" she asked with a smile.

He reached for his walker.

"Miss Benson said to take you in the wheelchair. I'll bring your walker in a few minutes."

Luke flipped through the pages of the tattered two-year-old *Readers Digest* someone had left in the examining room, and laid it aside when the doctor entered. He looked vaguely familiar.

He shook Luke's hand. "Dr. Brady, I'm Martin Brown. You may not remember me, but I was a student and then a resident under you about twelve years ago."

Luke's eyes widened in recognition. "Win." *Yes, I do remember you.*

"It's good to see you again. I just wish it was under different circumstances."

Luke nodded vigorously. *You and me both.*

Martin patted the examining table. "Could you get up here so I can check you?"

Luke noted Martin watched each movement as he hoisted himself up from the wheelchair and slowly pulled up onto the table. Martin made no move to assist but stood near enough to catch him if he slipped. He then methodically performed a thorough physical and neurological exam and watched again to see how well Luke maneuvered down from the table. Before he could sit down, Martin turned him toward the table and gently pushed him forward.

"I know you won't like it," he said while slipping on a glove, "but you'd dock my grade for sure if I didn't do a rectal exam. I remember your saying, 'If you don't put your finger in it, you're apt to put your foot in it.'"

Luke smiled. He was right. He just wished he hadn't been so attentive.

After Luke was back in his wheelchair, Martin pulled a chair from the desk and sat facing him.

"Dr. Brady, I've reviewed your case and talked with Dr. Harrelson. You know this as well as I do. It's been two months since your stroke. Statistically, you have regained from twenty to thirty percent of the function you will get back." He motioned toward the magazine. "Has your vision returned to normal?"

Luke nodded.

"With intensive physical and occupational therapy, I'm certain you'll be able to walk with a cane, maybe with no assistance at all. Your arm is more iffy. In time, you should be able to hit your mouth with a fork and handle a cane. I'm doubtful about writing with your right hand." He smiled. "As I recall your progress notes, that won't be too great a loss."

Luke laughed aloud, and quickly sobered. He'd have to keep trying. Despite the stroke, he now had almost as much strength in his right hand as in his left.

Martin hesitated, choosing his words. "We have an excellent speech therapist, but you've taken a major hit to your speech centers. I hope for some improvement, but I'm not optimistic. Dr. Harrelson feels the same. That's why he tried to get you in the experimental program."

Luke nodded. "Win." *You did that well, honest, and to the point with just a glimmer of hope.* He gave a wry smile. He had come to the same conclusions. But he was going to bust his chops to get better. He might just surprise them both.

Martin looked at his watch. "It's too late to go to therapy today, so nothing much will happen until Monday. Friday's not the best day to start anyway. That gives you two and a half days to get settled in and acquainted with the facility. Take it easy, and don't overdo it. They're going to push you hard. You need to be fresh."

Luke nodded.

Martin laid his notes beside the computer keyboard. "One more thing, Dr. Brady. I apologize. I never got around to thanking you."

Luke gave him a puzzled look.

"I'm a pretty good doctor, and, in large part, I owe that to you. I was the only African-American in my medical school and residency classes. Everyone wanted to have you for an instructor. I was on your service for every medical rotation the entire time. We both know that was no accident."

A faint smile flickered across Luke's face.

"You taught me the craft of medicine well, but you also taught me the art of medicine. For that I am forever grateful."

Luke touched Martin's arm. "Win." *Thank you. I needed that. From what I've seen, you learned well.*

⟫⟪

Luke returned to his room, flopped on his bed, and quickly dozed. Jimmy's spastic steps woke him.

Seeing Luke was awake, Jimmy pulled up a chair and sat down. They stared at each other.

"Why don't you like me?" Jimmy asked. He was near tears. This made his speech more choppy.

Luke spread his hands helplessly, pointed to his heart and then to Jimmy. "Win." *I'm so sorry.*

"Debbie says you can't talk. Can you?"

Luke shook his head.

"I talk kind of funny," Jimmy said. "Can you understand me?"

Another nod.

They sat not speaking for several minutes. Neither seemed bothered by the silence.

"I know you," Jimmy blurted. "You were my doctor. My mama—"

Luke held up his hand, halting him. He touched his own lips, then moved his hand slowly outward.

Jimmy frowned.

Luke repeated the gesture.

"Oh," Jimmy said, "you want me to talk slower."

Luke nodded. He was getting better at charades.

"When I was a little boy, my mama brought me to you." He hesitated. "You were nice. Anyway, I was in a special school for retarded kids. Mama told you I wasn't dumb. That I could read. You examined me, and then you and Mama got me into regular school."

I remember, Luke thought. She was tall and had long dark hair.

54

"You moved away several years later. I graduated. I was in the honor society, too. I still read a lot. I take college courses online."

Luke mentally kicked himself. He prided himself on being able to relate to others. He had started poorly here. "Win." *I'm sorry I'm kind of down.*

"What do you mean by 'win'?"

Luke struggled for some way to explain, then finally threw up his hands.

"Is that all you can say?"

Luke nodded.

Another long silence.

"Do you play chess?"

Luke shrugged.

"When we have time, we'll play. I read playing games helps people with strokes."

He was a lot smarter than Luke thought.

Jimmy looked at his watch. "I'll bet you're hungry. You slept through lunch." Luke shrugged.

"Come on. Let's go eat. Tonight is hamburger night. They're usually pretty good. Do you need a wheelchair?"

Luke shook his head and pulled his walker to the bedside. He pushed himself upright and started for the door, followed by Jimmy. He laughed out loud as scuffing and shuffling, herking and jerking, they trudged down the hall.

CHAPTER SIX

J immy snored softly. Luke glanced at his clock. Just past midnight. He flipped his pillow and pummeled it. Sleep flitted at the edge of his consciousness, but wouldn't light. Emotions—despair, hope, fear, anger—ricocheted around his brain. He even made a feeble attempt to pray. *God, I'm so frightened. Please help me.*

"May I come in?"

Luke jerked up, looking for the source of the voice. A dark figure strode from the doorway to his bedside.

"Win?" *Who are you?*

"I'm sorry," the stranger said. "I didn't mean to startle you. I heard a noise. I'm Father Gabe." He pointed to his photo identity tag.

He had dark curly hair cut short, almost military, deep-blue eyes crinkled at the corners, and a broad, friendly smile.

"Win." *What are you doing here?*

He ran his finger around his clerical collar. "I'm a priest. From time to time, I'm called to visit or share the sacraments with a parishioner."

He pulled up a chair. "My feet are complaining. Mind if I sit down for a few minutes?"

Luke shrugged. They sat staring at each other.

"Win." *Padre, I don't need you. I gave up on religion a long time ago.*

"Oh, did you? I could swear I heard you praying."

Suddenly Luke leaned forward, eyes squinting.

A faint smile flickered across Gabe's face.

"You understand what I said," Luke blurted.

"Why shouldn't I? You're speaking English."

"You don't know. I had a stroke. I can't talk. Nobody understands what I say," Luke said.

"I do."

"How?"

"Let's just say I'm good at languages," Gabe replied.

Luke struggled to grasp what was happening. "I'm not a parishioner. I'm not even Catholic." He paused. "Besides, God and I aren't on very good terms right now. Haven't been for some time."

"Do you want me to leave?"

"No! No, I'm just frustrated and angry."

Gabe pulled his chair closer. "Angry about what?"

"I'll tell you what. After twenty-four years of concentrated effort, I was appointed dean of the medical school. I worked so hard to get there. I had such big plans. Now my universe is one brick building on two acres of land in the middle of nowhere. Father, I tried it your way from the time I was a kid. Now I can't talk. I can barely walk. I can't practice medicine. I can't teach. Where's the fairness in that?"

"Whoever said life was fair?"

"Well...I..." Luke stammered.

"Other than a brief twinge of pity, how deeply did you consider the fairness to all those 'interesting' cases—those poor benighted souls with gosh-awful, life-disrupting diseases—you so carefully demonstrated to your students?"

Luke drew back, stunned. "I really tried to help them, to treat them with understanding." His gaze fell. "I guess I did slip up a lot."

Gabe laid his hand on Luke's arm. "I'm not condemning you. You tried. Most of the time you did fine."

"How would you know?"

"I'm very intuitive."

"So, what do I do now?"

"What are your priorities? What's important in your life?"

Luke gave a brief laugh. "I once wrote an essay on that very topic."

"What did it say?"

Luke stared into the darkness. "I said the four most important things in my life were God, my family, medicine, and me—in that order."

"Is that how you lived?"

"I tried. But if I'm honest, for the last twenty-five years I reversed the order."

Gabe said nothing.

Luke looked him directly in the eye. "Then God dumped on me, my family left me, and now I've lost medicine." He shrugged. "What if I never talk again? What's left for me?"

"That's up to you. I'm sure He's still got some important use for you."

"I'd like to know what it is."

"Think about it. Think hard about it."

Gabe rose to leave.

"Don't go. I think you're full of baloney, but it feels so good to hear my voice outside my head."

"I must go."

"Will you come back?"

"The next time I'm in the building, I'll be sure and stop in," he said as he strode out the door.

Luke looked over where Jimmy slept undisturbed.

He couldn't lie still. What just happened? It couldn't have been real. He hoped it was just a realistic dream. If not, he was taking advice from a hallucination. Just what he needed. Adding mental illness to all his other problems. What next?

He began to choke up. He slapped himself—hard. *Snap out of it, Luke. Pity doesn't become you. You pulled through a rougher time than this. You can do it again, God or no God. Just suck it up and get to work. Who knows how much you may improve?*

CHAPTER SEVEN

Luke woke from his after-lunch nap. Jimmy sat quietly reading his Bible. He set it aside when Luke sat up.

"Would you like me to show you around?" Jimmy asked.

It took Luke a moment to decipher his speech. Then he nodded and reached for his walker.

"It may take a while." Jimmy said with a short laugh. "Neither of us moves very fast."

Every muscle in Jimmy's body was stiff and spastic except his dark brown eyes. Despite a permanent squint, they were alive and noticed everything. When he stood, he tilted forward. Combined with his bent knees and elbows and splayed fingers, this gave him the appearance of a giant praying mantis.

First stop was the kitchen. "Maybelle," he said to the cook, "this is Dr. Brady." He looked at the large tray of brownies. "We always have brownies for dessert on Saturday nights." He gave Maybelle an expectant look.

She sighed in mock exasperation. "OK, Jimmy, just one. Here's one for you, Dr. Brady. If I were you, I'd be careful about associating with panhandlers. Not good for your reputation."

The halls were lined with people in rolling chairs with trays like school desks that served mainly to keep them semierect and prevent their escape—no different from twenty-five years ago. Who knows, they might be the same chairs. The background odor of urine with an occasional whiff of feces was unchanged also.

Debbie struggled to straighten an obese man in a table-chair.

"Here let me help you," Jimmy said. Together they pulled him upright.

"Thank you," Debbie said and smiled.

Jimmy blushed.

"She's the prettiest girl I've ever seen," Jimmy said when they walked away.

Luke looked closer. She was attractive: medium height, trim, short brunet hair. Her most striking feature was her face: deep-brown eyes and a smile that seemed to shout, "I am so happy."

"Here's the activity room," Jimmy said. The bushy-haired lady in the wheelchair was planted in front of the TV. "That's Pauline," Jimmy said. "If watching TV was as bad for your eyes as they say, she'd be blind."

Pauline glared at him and frowned.

Jimmy pointed to the dining room as they passed. "After meals, the back part is the recreation area. There's always coffee in the urn in the corner. They have church there on Sunday." He led Luke into the next room. "This is physical therapy. Nobody's here on weekends."

Luke wandered around the room. The basic equipment was all there. Not as up-to-date or shiny as at the university rehab center but serviceable.

As they meandered through the patient areas, many of the residents spoke to Jimmy.

"That's the Alzheimer's and dementia unit." Jimmy nodded toward a side hallway. "I don't like to go there. It makes me sad."

Luke pushed his walker through the door. The odor of body waste was stronger. A gaunt woman confined to her rolling desk chair, held out her hands and screeched an incoherent babble. Luke made his way to her, knelt, and gently took one of her hands in his good left hand. He smiled and looked her directly in the eye. As he held her hand, the screeching and babbling waned and finally stopped. Her wild expression softened, and she smiled at him. She was still smiling when they left.

"This is the first time I've ever seen her quiet," Jimmy said as they exited the unit. He motioned to Luke. "This way. I want to show you something, but don't tell anyone."

With a bemused look, Luke motioned as if locking his lips.

Jimmy led him down a short hallway, into the trash room, and through an exit into the courtyard. "This door is never locked. A lot of the people come here to smoke. When it's warm, I like to sit here at night and look at the stars. Sit down. I'll be right back."

He retrieved a sack of birdseed from the trash room and re-filled the feeder hanging from the maple tree.

"They said I could have it if I took care of it."

They sat without speaking, watching chickadees, titmice and juncos swarm about.

What don't you do around here? Luke thought.

✥

His days fell into a settled routine: Physical therapy, nine to ten. Paul, the therapist, was good, as good as the ones at university rehab. The main difference was the lack of support staff. He had two aides, as opposed to the myriad therapists, therapy students, and aides at the university. He pushed Luke hard. "Come on, Doc. Pick it up. No pain, no gain. You want to get out of here?"

Occupational therapy, ten thirty to eleven thirty. Same story, more-than-competent therapist with no help. She was, however, pleased to have a patient as eager to improve as Luke.

A frustrating hour of speech therapy followed lunch. As at university rehab, there was no progress.

A boring afternoon of no planned activity ensued.

Dinner served to break the torpor stretching until bedtime. Most days he and Jimmy played chess and walked the length of the four hallways. The rehabilitation wing had a fairly rapid turnover of patients. Most had broken hips and minor strokes and were in and out in three to six weeks. The custodial care and dementia wings were another matter. Clustered across the hall from the nurses' station was a gaggle of high-backed desk chairs on rollers with occupants lolling in varying stages of alertness. Most of them seldom had visitors. With the exception of being rolled to the dining room for meals, a morning bath, and changes of diapers, their days were spent staring or babbling to themselves. Residents who were bedfast were even more isolated.

A lady with stringy red hair was a regular at the intersection of Wing Three and Wing Four. She looked vaguely familiar.

"Hi ya, Doc," she greeted them as they passed by. "See ya, Doc," she chimed on their return trip. The first time Luke smiled, nodded, and gave Jimmy a questioning look.

"That's Myrtle Langhorn," Jimmy said. "She's confused a lot of the time. You used to be her doctor. Debbie says she remembers you."

She repeated her salutations without fail on each of their trips.

In many ways, Shadydale was not much different from a minimum security prison. The doors were alarmed to prevent residents from "eloping." Despite the busy routine of therapy, Shadydale's version of compulsory exercise, there remained hours of idle time. Mealtimes provided the only break in the constant monotony—a monotony made worse on weekends when there was no therapy.

Waiting for Monday was Shadydale's equivalent of being on hold for the IRS help line. The only difference was the lack of elevator music and someone to tell you every two minutes how important your call was. The sole bright spot was Julie's visit every Saturday afternoon.

Compounding the tedious sameness was an almost total lack of solitude. Except for the chapel, time alone was almost impossible within the confines of Shadydale.

⛓⛓

The nurses' station clock stood at 4:37. Most activity at Shadydale had ceased by 9:00 p.m. Consequently, Luke was asleep by 10:00 and woke around 4:00 a.m., even earlier than Jimmy. This quiet, early respite from the intrusive daily bustle was a welcome relief.

He smiled and nodded to the nurses, then continued up the hall to the activity area of the darkened dining room. He clicked the lamp beside the recliner next to a large bookcase to which was attached a sign: Library. A local church kept it stocked with bibles, inspirational books, and a few well-worn best sellers. Most were large print editions. Luke settled into the recliner and opened a *New England Journal*.

He looked up at the sound of squeaking shoes crossing the darkened room. A tall white-clad form materialized in his circle of light. Miss Benson, the queen bee. He smiled at the thought.

"What's so funny, *Dr.* Brady?" Her voice was flat and hard.

He struggled to sit up straight.

"Don't bother."

He slumped back. "Win." *What do you want?*

"Win." She gave a brief laugh. "What the hell does that mean? I don't understand you."

Arms crossed, she towered over him.

"You don't remember me, do you?"

He studied her face and shook his head.

"I'm sure I was a nobody to you. Fifteen years ago. University Hospital. Night charge nurse, ICU. I was Martha Fletcher then."

His eyes widened. Nurse Fletcher. Yes. Her hair had been brighter red then, but she was the same full-breasted, statuesque beauty who turned the heads of all the male staff. Same tight, long-sleeved sweater. Yes, he remembered. He had walked in on her in the medication room injecting herself with Demerol. He reported her. An investigation found large quantities of narcotics missing. She had falsely documented giving them to patients. He never saw her again.

"Yes, you do remember, Dr. Holier-than-Thou. I begged you not to report me. I promised never to do it again. But no, you were the hotshot young instructor, the rising star. You made an example of me to enhance your reputation."

"Win." *I had no choice.*

"You never asked why. I'll tell you. I was under unbearable stress. Directing ICU wasn't enough. I was also supporting a worthless husband and two kids. The drugs kept me going."

She snuffed her nose and swabbed her tears, smearing her makeup.

"Do you know what happened to me? I'm sure you never checked. While you were becoming rich and famous, I lost my license—for a whole year. After it was reinstated, the only job I could get was in this jerkwater nursing home, caring for invalids like you and humping the administrator for a raise. I lost my husband. And…and…I lost my children. His lawyer got me declared an unfit mother. I saw them on holidays and every other weekend. When they were old enough to choose, they chose him. I haven't seen or heard from them in six years." She clenched her fists. "It's all your fault."

He shook his head. "Win." *I'm so sorry. I didn't realize.*

She leaned closer, her face not six inches from his.

"Win, my ass! I swore I'd get even, and now I will. I promise, you will never leave Shadydale. Who's in charge now, Dr. Bigshot?"

The pupils of her eyes were pinpoints. *My God, she's still using.*

She spun around, and shoes squeaking, she disappeared into the darkness.

His journal lay unnoticed in his lap. Stunned and shaken, he stared into the darkness, trying to process what had just happened. He strained to remember, but he could recollect nothing else about the episode. How could he have known what a devastating chain of events he had set in motion? What if he had worked with her? What should he do now? What could he do now? How serious were her threats? Would she follow through?

Later, in the dining room, her makeup was again perfect. As she passed him, she smiled sweetly and winked.

⊶⊷

"Come on, Dr. Brady," Jimmy said, "tonight's spaghetti night. It's the best meal of the week."

"Hi ya, Doc," Myrtle greeted him at the door.

Luke smiled and nodded.

Cursing his clumsy right hand, Luke stabbed at the elusive spaghetti strands with his fork. Jimmy had wolfed his food down and now kept up a running commentary.

"They call themselves the wheezer geezers." Jimmy pointed to a group at a table against the wall. Three emaciated men in wheelchairs labored to eat while continuing to breathe. Plastic tubes ran from oxygen tanks to their noses. A fourth, overweight with blue lips, wheezed audibly between bites. "They smoke on the courtyard unless it rains. If it's raining, they just sit around belching, cussing, and telling dirty jokes."

Jimmy nodded toward a circle of seven women and two men seated in large trayed chairs. There were two such circles in the dining area.

"They're the dementias and Alzheimer's."

Each tray held a dish of pureed food. An aide in the center of the circle spooned the glop into their mouths, first one, then the next, and the next, then repeat. A loud fart erupted from one followed by a soupy gurgle.

"Thar she blows," one of the geezers whooped. His partners' guffaws foundered abruptly on a stormy shoal of wheezing, hacking, and coughing.

Luke pushed his food away as the sweet-sour fecal odor ubiquitous to nursing homes wafted from the circle, insidiously spreading throughout the room. He remembered the medical students' name for it, Eau de Crappe.

"Dammit, Ellie," her aide snapped and yanked a can of air freshener from the food cart. She sprayed the entire area—residents, food, and all. No one except the geezers seemed to notice or look up from their meal.

"That's Bill and Tillie, the lovebirds." Jimmy motioned to an elderly couple at a table in the corner. They leaned toward each other, talking and laughing. "Sometimes at night, he sneaks into her room."

Table by table Jimmy continued his commentary, introducing Luke to his fellow inmates in this institute for the infirm.

Jimmy was something else. He was familiar with everyone. Food seemed to obsess him. He knew the daily menus by heart. He cadged cookies, ice cream, and a variety of desserts from the kitchen crew or the nurses every evening and often during the day. Despite his prodigious appetite, he remained slender.

Luke sat in his recliner, idly gazing out the window. He had been in Shadydale six weeks. Jimmy's Sunday paper lay unread in his lap. Faint snatches of hymns wafted down the hallway from the church service in the dining hall. Jimmy never missed. Luke abstained despite Jimmy's urging him to attend. This was the only planned activity of the weekend, leaving the residents to their own devices for occupying the rest of their time. A few minutes later, the doxology signaled the end of the service.

Jimmy rushed in. "Dr. Brady, I'm going out for the afternoon—you be OK?"

Luke smiled and nodded.

Every summer when Luke was a child, his family spent a week at his grandparents' in a poor section of Atlanta. Seven tedious, hot, humid days sleeping on a pallet of quilts, cooled only by an oscillating fan. No air conditioner, no TV, and no one to play with. He wasn't allowed out of the yard because it was a "bad section" of town. All the adults did was sit around, talk, eat, take naps, and play dominos. Before leaving Valdosta, he checked four books from the library. If he selected well, this provided hours of distraction, but a fellow could only read so much. By the end of the week, he was reduced to enticing doodlebugs from their burrows with a broom straw.

Weekends at Shadydale were more boring than childhood Atlanta, especially when Jimmy wasn't there. Today he was on his own.

When he practiced in Buxton, he visited Shadydale as seldom as possible. As a solo practitioner, his schedule was tight. He had to prioritize his time: emergency room patients first, followed by hospital patients, office patients, phone calls to patients, and paperwork, in that order. Family time and Shadydale claimed the few remaining hours. Shadydale always came in last. He came only when insurance or concerned nurses required. This happened all too often for him. He signed the forms, treated the patients, and vacated the premises as quickly as possible, knowing full well he was doing shoddy work.

Today he wandered the halls and saw with the eyes of a patient and not a harried physician. He quickly realized his two months at university rehab were an aberration. With its superior funding and staffing, university rehab was the exception among nursing homes. Shadydale was the rule. Like the pyramids, Grand Canyon, and government bureaucracy, nothing about Shadydale ever changed.

Immediately upon leaving the lobby and business area, the new or infrequent visitor was slapped in the face by the pervasive odor of feces, urine, and ineffective air freshener. Residents, patients, and workers barely noticed. Their nostrils had become desensitized.

Although not as polished and shiny as university rehab, Shadydale was clean. The housekeeping staff was almost entirely Hispanic. Few locals would do this work for the low wages they received. They treated anyone with the least appearance of authority with exaggerated deference. They scurried about with their mops, buckets, and armloads of linens nearly unnoticed. They spoke little and kept their gazes averted, as if just making eye contact would result in immediate deportation.

LPNs and nurses' aides were overwhelmingly kind and dedicated. Few who did not love old people would work as hard and for as little pay as they did. At the rehab center, most of the nurses' aides were young prenursing students. Here, the majority were middle-aged women who were accustomed to tending elderly parents and relatives. They took these skills to work with them; their caring and compassion more than made up for their lack of formal training.

Most of the nurses worked here for the same reasons as the aides. Although Martha Benson appeared to be here because she had nowhere else to go, she was a good nurse and administrator.

She might be weak in interpersonal skills, but her nursing staff was professional and well trained. He was impressed she taught continuing education classes for RNs and LPNs each Tuesday and aides every Thursday. The weekend charge nurse repeated these classes for those who worked only Saturday or Sunday. Even the reduced weekend staff functioned smoothly.

Although he hated being here, Luke had to admit, despite the lack of frills, Shadydale was competently run.

Like the rest of Shadydale, the food was not up to rehab center standards but was acceptable. Maybelle made the most with what she had.

Saturday and Sunday lunches were the two best meals of the week, probably intended to impress visitors and families, as if this was the typical fare for their loved ones. It was not.

The rest of the meals were not bad, but neither were they special in any way.

Toast, scrambled eggs, and bacon alternated with oatmeal to comprise weekday breakfasts. Perhaps for visitors' view, omelets were served on Saturday and waffles on Sunday. Included with each breakfast—even with oatmeal—was a generous dollop of grits.

Noon and evening meals also catered to the rural southern tastes of most of the residents. Staples such as turnip greens, pinto beans, black-eyed peas, fried okra, and corn bread formed the basic dietary offerings and were served with taste-numbing regularity.

Entrees consisted of fried chicken, fried pork chops, sauerkraut and wieners, macaroni and cheese with ham, and, most often of all, something Jimmy called mystery meat—high in fat and protein but low in taste. Twice a week they served his favorites—spaghetti or hamburgers.

Thanksgiving dinner had been spectacular—turkey, dressing, sweet potato casserole, green beans, yeast rolls, and pecan pie— with enough left over for supper.

⇥┼⇤

Today was special. Instead of her usual one-hour Saturday visit, Julie stayed four. Ebullient over her team's victory the night before, she gave him a play-by-play recount. She gave an equally excited description of her pregnancy. Finally, she rose to go.

She kissed Luke. "Goodbye, Daddy. See you next Saturday." She turned to Jimmy. "You make sure he behaves and works hard at his therapy. Oh, thank you for the cookies."

After she left, Jimmy quietly began his Bible study. Luke picked up his medical journal and resumed an article on advances in diabetic care—dull, but anything to ward off the Saturday afternoon blues for a while.

Thirty minutes later, Jimmy shut his Bible.

"Want to walk before supper?" he asked.

Luke nodded and grasped his walker.

They had made the entire circuit of Shadydale twice when they saw a flurry of activity at room 317.

"That's Bill Fredricks's room," Jimmy said. "You remember, the love bird."

Before he could say more, two men in dark suits wheeled out a gurney bearing a bulging black body bag.

"Too bad," Jimmy said. "He was real nice."

They continued toward the dining room.

"The undertaker comes here more often than the meter man," Jimmy said.

CHAPTER EIGHT

Luke stared into the darkness. Why had he done it? Why had he agreed to go to church with Jimmy tomorrow morning? Since his first week at Shadydale, Jimmy had been bugging him to go to church with him. In the afterglow of Julie's visit, he had agreed.

As far back as he could remember, he had attended church—twice on Sundays and on Wednesday night. As in much of the South, his family's social life revolved around church. Even today, after much neglect, he could still quote large sections of scripture from memory. Helen came from the same tradition. After their marriage, they followed a similar pattern of worship. The move to Atlanta changed that. Helen dropped church entirely. He attended only for weddings and funerals. Had it just been a habit he slipped out of? Had he been trying to get back at God? Whatever his reasoning, uneasiness gripped him. Sometime after two, he fell into a fitful sleep.

Jimmy chattered through breakfast.

"You're in luck. Father Ryan is here today. He's Episcopalian." It took him two tries to enunciate the multisyllabic denomination. "He teaches good things. Not like Preacher Wilkens. He scares people, yelling about sin and hellfire. He makes some of the dementias cry. Or Reverend Seiber. He talks funnier than me. He gives a little grunt after every phrase." Jimmy laughed. "Like he's rapping God."

Tables had been cleared from half the dining room. A wooden lectern stood by the piano. Two groups of chairs were arranged in ten rows with four chairs to a row. A hymnal lay in each chair.

Luke and Jimmy arrived first. Luke took the rear seat nearest the door.

"I usually sit up front," Jimmy said, his voice tinged with disappointment. Luke didn't budge.

A middle-aged woman sat at the piano and softly played a medley of hymns as the residents filed in. The room filled quickly. Patients in wheelchairs were placed on either side. In keeping with Shadydale's demographics, the congregation was mostly female. A good number drowsed or looked around with blank stares.

Father Ryan greeted everyone and said a short prayer, followed by a brief homily on God's love and presence in all circumstances, even illness, and in all places, even nursing homes.

Easy for you to say, Luke thought. *You're healthy, live at home, and are free as a bird.* His mood soured even more. Why had he let Jimmy persuade him to come?

Father Ryan closed with another prayer. A young man stepped to the lectern.

"Good morning," he said cheerfully.

"Good morning," a smattering of residents replied.

"Please turn to hymn number one seventy-one, 'What a Friend We Have in Jesus.'"

"What a friend we have in Jesus, all our sins and griefs to bear..."

The volume of their singing resounded throughout the room. Luke watched with surprised interest. Almost everyone sang, but few used a hymnal. Even more surprising, many who had been drowsing and a few of the dementia patients belted out every song, even the less familiar third stanzas. From somewhere deep in their flawed brains, the words and tunes squirreled away by a lifetime of repetition burst forth.

Jimmy's hymnal was open, but he seldom referred to it. If not for the spasticity of his throat, he might have had a pleasant tenor voice. He kept up fairly well on the slower pieces but stumbled on livelier tunes such as "Standing on the Promises."

Luke found himself humming along with them.

After the last words of "Onward Christian Soldiers" faded, the song leader said, "Let's close with 'Amazing Grace,' page two forty-six."

Luke hummed enthusiastically. "I once was lost, but now am found, was blind, but now I see."

Jimmy's head snapped around as Luke's rich baritone rang out. "Dr. Brady, you talked!"

Luke was too stunned to continue humming. Whenever he had tried to talk, he never heard the "win" everyone claimed he said. Since his stroke, he heard words only in his head. But he had heard these words loud and clear.

⟞⟨⊹ ⊹⟩⟝

After lunch, Luke sat alone in the privacy of the chapel, contemplating what had happened. Before this morning, the only time he had actually heard his voice since his stroke was when he talked with the mysterious Father Gabe.

He had never encountered one, but he had heard reports of stroke and brain-injured patients with aphasia who were able to sing conversations rather than speak them. What if he could do that, too? This could be his ticket back to university rehab. Maybe even back to teaching. He laughed. He could see it now, the singing professor.

He opened the hymnal he had taken from the stack by the piano. He hummed as he read the lines of "Amazing Grace." The words were clear in his mind, but he heard nothing.

＝＜┼┼＞＝

The next morning at breakfast, Jimmy fetched Martin.

"Dr. Brown, Dr. Brady talked…no, Dr. Brady sang out loud yesterday at church," he said.

Martin listened to Jimmy's rendition of what had happened.

"I've heard of cases where stroke patients could sing things they couldn't say," he said. "I've never seen such a case, but I'll research it."

Luke pointed his finger at himself.

Martin looked puzzled.

Luke motioned, taking something from Martin, then pointed to himself.

"I think he wants you to bring the reports to him," Jimmy said.

Luke nodded vigorously.

"Give me a few days," Martin said.

Jimmy found Luke at lunch.

Luke was elated. He devoured his food. To Jimmy's disappointment, he didn't share his dessert as usual.

Luke rose and motioned for Jimmy to come with him. Together they went to speech therapy. Jimmy repeated what he had told Martin. The therapist was equally surprised and unfamiliar with the situation. She promised to call a consultant and get information for Luke.

"Dr. Brady, I'm slow on the computer, but I'm really good," Jimmy said. "Dr. Martin gave me some keywords. I'll see if I can find some things for you, too."

———

Luke plunged into his speech therapy with renewed vigor. The therapist played CDs of hymns and familiar songs and provided Luke with the lyrics. Luke hummed along and at unpredictable times a phrase or two—sometimes an entire verse—burst out. His singing reminded him of the old TV sing-along shows, but instead of following the bouncing ball, he could sing only in response to others and only then with whatever fragments remained in his brain's musical circuits.

He read and reread more than one hundred studies of patients with aphasia who could communicate by singing rather than speaking. There were no case reports of patients with losses as severe as his. Almost all dealt with patients who could speak words to some degree. Most had problems with finding the right word or speaking words in the right sequence. One theory was once words were formed in the mind, singing followed a different pathway to articulation than speaking did.

Luke concluded he had no problem finding correct words or sequences. Whatever oral expression he had, came not from his ideation, but from bits and pieces of tunes stored deep in his memory. He could sing only what was buried in his subconscious mind. Hearing others sing them must somehow send them along a different neural track than normal speech. Once he sang the remembered fragment, it was gone. He couldn't voluntarily resurrect it. That required another audible trigger. He could read the words and hum the tune, but without the audible trigger, nothing happened. Each time they sang "Amazing Grace" in church, he sang the last part of the first stanza. Each time it surprised him as much as when it first happened.

Luke became a regular at Sunday morning services, enduring Preacher Wilson's shouts and Reverend Seiber's grunts on the chance he might sing a phrase or two. Was this a form of worship, crass opportunism, or sacrilege? He didn't know. He didn't care.

He had always been partial to instrumental music, but now he used Jimmy's laptop to listen to golden oldies on Sirius. He'd hum along, and without warning, a snippet of song would erupt. Once, he and Jimmy sat before their TV, drinking colas and eating popcorn, waiting for an NFL game to begin. Luke hummed along with a pop singer who was desecrating the national anthem.

"Ahhh!" Jimmy yelled and strewed his popcorn across the room when Luke boomed "and the home of the brave."

The chapel had become Luke's favorite predawn refuge. Jimmy never bothered him there. Neither did Martha Benson. He wondered if this was some superstition on her part. Today he felt the urge to pray. He should be thankful, he thought. Hearing his voice, if only for a few moments, raised his spirits. But where did God get off toying with him like a cat with a mouse? Raising his hopes this development might lead back to some semblance of the life he had lost, then dashing them. Could he be grateful and angry at the same time about the same thing? Where was Father Gabe when he needed him? He started to rise, paused for a moment, and bowed his head.

"Thanks...I guess."

After three weeks of no new progress, the therapist put away the CDs and again began plodding along with traditional speech therapy. Luke continued to hum along with the radio and at church. He found he could sing bits and pieces of other hymns and songs. But he always sang the same fragments from the same song and could not recruit one new word, even from the same verse. After six weeks of concerted effort, he concluded his singing was a pleasant diversion, but nothing more.

CHAPTER NINE

*I*n *the beginning God created the heaven and the earth.* Luke read the line smoothly despite the shaky, crude lettering. He gave a scornful snort. Before the stroke, his writing was barely legible using a good right hand. Now it was hieroglyphics, and poor hieroglyphics at that.

The speech therapist was convinced he would never speak again. She and the occupational therapist had devised an exercise to see if he could write his thoughts rather than speak them. Find a familiar text. Copy it. Then cover it and rewrite it from memory.

He closed the Bible and laid it over his copy. *In the beginning God created the heaven and the earth.* The line flowed easily in his head. Now he tried to write it. His fingers blanched as he willed the pencil to write.

In...

He forced the pencil to move, creating a squiggly line.

In...

Perspiration beaded his forehead. The lead snapped as he elongated the line.

He slammed the pencil down.

He could recite the Gettysburg Address and the Twenty-Third Psalm in his head, but he couldn't transmit a simple "In" to his vocal cords or his hand. To hell with it.

He raked his hand, knocking the Bible, pencil, and papers to the floor, and he pounded the table.

Jimmy laid his newspaper aside and awkwardly knelt, gathered the articles, and returned them to Luke's table. He examined the writing and squiggles.

"You can't write what you're thinking, either?"

Luke shook his head.

Jimmy returned to his chair, lost in thought.

Luke shuffled to his recliner, flopped down, shut his eyes, and tried to relax.

"Dr. Brady."

Luke ignored him and pretended to doze.

"Dr. Brady."

Luke sighed and looked up.

What do you want, Jimmy?

"Can you do math?"

Luke nodded.

"What's one plus one?"

Rolling his eyes, Luke held up two fingers.

"Can you say it?"

Luke strained for the elusive "two" but produced only a frustrated, squeaky "Win."

"What's two times two?"

Four fingers.

Jimmy handed him a fresh pencil and a piece of paper.

"Write this down. One plus one equals two."

Resigned, but intrigued, Luke wrote: 1+1=2.

Just like that. No problem.

"What's three times seven?"

Luke wrote again, shaky, but there it was: 3x7=21. His heart skipped.

That's amazing. He couldn't say the numbers or transmit their names to his hand, but he could do the math and convey the symbols. Jimmy was something else.

"I read about strokes on the Internet. It said solving puzzles helps your brain.

Luke nodded. How many times had he told that to patients?

"I know a math puzzle," Jimmy said. "Would you rather get one hundred dollars a day for thirty days or get a penny, double it, and continue to double the results daily for thirty days?"

Luke wrote 100.

"Wrong!" Jimmy clapped his hands and laughed.

Luke gave him a scornful look.

"Work it out," Jimmy said and returned to his newspaper.

A smile crept across Luke's face.

That's just how he would handle it with a first-year medical student. *Jimmy, you'd make a good instructor.*

He spent over an hour, laboriously writing, checking, and rechecking his figures. He grunted, and Jimmy came over.

$5,368,709.12.

"That's right." He hesitated. "I know you're a very smart man, but you shouldn't make snap judgments about anything—math, or what you might or might not be able to accomplish. I know."

He went to the chest at the foot of his bed, opened it, and lifted a framed diploma from the University of Georgia, followed by a framed CPA license.

"I got them through online correspondence courses." He laughed. "It wasn't hard, but it took me seven years." He paused a moment, then held up his spastic, contorted hands, his comedic timing perfect. "I type real slow."

Luke burst out laughing.

"If I can do it, so can you."

Luke studied Jimmy's sincere face and contorted body. He was smart, but he was also sensitive and kind. He reminded Luke of his patients with Down syndrome. Even though mentally and physically challenged, to a person they were kind and caring. It seemed as if the deleted chromosome fragment bore with it their genes for meanness. Perhaps the lack of oxygen that devastated the muscular control areas of Jimmy's brain also asphyxiated his mean center.

⟨+ +⟩

Jimmy and Debbie sat at a corner table in the dining room, sipping hot chocolate as they did each Wednesday. Every other day she left directly after her shift to attend the registered nurses program at the local community college. Debbie was a petite brunet with dark-brown eyes. Jimmy watched her with a smitten gaze as she quietly talked.

She nodded to the corner table where a disheveled gray-haired lady in a rumpled bathrobe picked at her food. She was barely recognizable as the lovebird Jimmy had pointed out to Luke.

"Do you think you could get Dr. Brady to see Tillie?" she asked. "She barely gets out of her room since Bill died."

"What could he do?" Jimmy said. "He can't talk."

"I'm not sure he can do anything, but she's from Buxton. Maybe she knew him from before."

"I don't know, but I'll try."

⟨+ +⟩

Jimmy tapped on the door.

"Come in."

Tillie sat in a wicker chair by the window. Her knitting lay on her lap. Her listless eyes and barely combed hair were at odds with her elegant bearing.

"I'm so sorry about Bill," Jimmy said.

"Thank you, Jimmy." She looked uncertainly at Luke.

"This is Dr. Brady. He was my doctor in Buxton a long time ago."

"He was my sister's doctor. She told me about him." She nodded to Luke. "Won't you sit down, Doctor?"

Luke pulled a chair near and sat facing her.

"Dr. Brady can't talk, but he understands what you say," Jimmy said. He shifted from one foot to the other. "Well, I've got to go," he said and left.

Tillie gave a wan smile. "Jimmy's a very sweet boy."

Luke nodded.

She sat silently, first staring out the window, then at the knitting. Her chin began to quiver and a stray tear coursed down her cheek.

"I was knitting Bill a sweater. He was always cold."

Luke lifted the wool fabric from her lap and examined it. He smiled, nodded in approval, and placed it back in her lap.

He motioned to a picture on her bedside table. Younger, but still radiantly beautiful in her wedding gown, she stood by a tall man with slicked-down black hair.

"That's Matthew, my husband. We were married for fifty-one years. He died four years ago. Three months later my daughter put me here rather than let me live alone. She lives in Oregon. I hated it at first."

He smiled and tapped his chest.

"Yes, I imagine you do, too."

She paused, then continued.

"I didn't know anyone here who wasn't demented. Sarah has only returned to see me twice. I was miserable. Then Bill came."

Her voice became more animated. "He and his wife, Jenny, had been friends of Matthew and me for years. About fifteen years ago, they moved to Ohio. Jenny died ten years later. Three years ago,

Bill had a heart attack and moved back here to live with his son. They didn't get along, so he put Bill here into Shadydale. We resumed our friendship. He made life worth living again."

She bit her lip.

"You'll hear about it sooner or later. We became lovers."

He squeezed her hand and nodded.

"Yes, it was good."

She talked for over an hour.

"Look at the time. My, how I've run on." She patted her hair. "I've let myself go. I must look a sight. I need to freshen up before dinner."

When Luke stood, she took his hand.

"Thank you for coming. It's been so nice talking to you. Please come again."

⊱⊰

"Look at Tillie," Jimmy said.

Her hair and makeup were perfect. She smiled at them as she strode by to their accustomed table in the corner.

83

CHAPTER TEN

Luke and Jimmy ambled down the Wing Three hallway. There was little else to do on a Saturday morning.

"Hiya—" Myrtle's customary greeting ended in a fit of coughing.

Luke stopped and bent over her. She forced a smile. Her lips were blue, as were her nail beds. Her pulse was 122, and she was breathing twenty-eight times a minute. He knelt and inspected her legs. Her right calf was swollen, and she winced when he squeezed it. Luke strode to the nurses' station.

"Good morning, Dr. Brady," the nurse said.

He pointed to Myrtle.

"She developed a cold last night."

He shook his head and motioned for her to follow him. He held up Myrtle's blue finger and made a pinching motion on her fingertip.

"What do you want, Dr. Brady?"

He repeated the motion and panted, pointing to his chest.

"I don't understand," she said.

"I think he wants you to check her oxygen," Jimmy said.

She retrieved the pulse oximeter and clipped it on Myrtle's finger.

"Oh my gosh!" she exclaimed. It read eighty-four. "What should I do?"

Luke hurried back to the nurses' station. He pointed to the phone.

"You want me to call Dr. Brown?"

Luke nodded vigorously.

━╬━━

"Dr. Brady, you probably saved Myrtle's life," Martin said. "We'll get a lung scan Monday to confirm it, but I'm sure she has phlebitis and has thrown some pulmonary emboli." He noted Jimmy's puzzled look. "Clots to her lungs. I've put her at bed rest, and now that the blood thinner is started, I'm sure she'll be OK. I doubt she'd have made it through the weekend without it."

━╬━━

Three days later, Martin strolled to Luke and Jimmy's table carrying his usual lunch, an apple and a cup of coffee.

"Good afternoon. Mind if I join you?" he asked.

"No, sit. Sit," Jimmy replied.

"I'm due back at the office, but I wanted to talk to you, Dr. Brady."

Luke nodded.

"I was really impressed with how you dealt with Myrtle," he said. "She's doing fine, by the way."

"We know," Jimmy said. "We check on her every day."

"That figures," Martin said with a smile, "and it goes to an idea I had. You can really help me."

Luke raised his eyebrows. *How?*

85

He looked directly at Luke. "Dr. Brady, you're still an exceptional doctor. Your license is still active. Practicing alone, as I do, it's easy to let things slip. I really need someone to bounce things off of, someone to go over tough cases with. You could look over my shoulder, catch what I miss, and give me advice when I need it. We can be finished before your therapy begins."

Luke was nodding his head in vigorous agreement even before Martin finished.

"I don't want to overload you, but if the nurses could have you evaluate patients when they have concerns and call me if you think they should, it would benefit the patients, and be a huge help to me. The nurses think this is a great idea."

Again Luke nodded his head.

"Jimmy, if you would, I'd like for you to come with us. You can handle the charts and interpret when I can't understand Dr. Brady."

Jimmy beamed. He and Luke had developed a workable communication system consisting of a combination of signs, expressions, and pantomime.

"Great, we'll start in the morning. I'll try to get here around seven thirty."

He rose to leave. Luke grasped his arm, then, Gandhi-like, put his hands together and bowed his head.

"He says thank you," Jimmy said.

Martin looked Luke directly in the eye. "No, thank you."

⚊⚌⚌

"Aren't you the early bird," Amy said. "Five a.m. If there's a worm to be had, it's yours."

Luke chuckled.

"Dr. Brown told me you would be rounding with him," she said. "He can use the help. Before you get started, I'd like you to meet

Rachel Graham, a local girl who's come home. She's the new night charge nurse."

Rachel shook his hand with a firm grip that surprised him. "I'm glad to meet you, Dr. Brady," she said with a dimpled smile that lit up the nurses' station.

Luke smiled, nodded, and with a questioning look, pointed at Amy.

"Me? I'm going to be the day shift charge nurse starting Monday. I think that's a promotion."

Luke smiled and gave her thumbs-up. After one last look at Rachel, he collected his charts.

"You have a busy morning: two new admissions and five recerts," Amy said.

Luke scanned the charts, then pushed the cart down the hall. He was on the last chart when he heard Jimmy's slapping, scraping steps.

"Let's get breakfast before Dr. Brown comes," Jimmy said.

⊁⊹⊱

"I expected you to shadow me, not do my job," Martin said. "I'm not complaining, you understand," he said with a smile.

Martin signed the recerts, then went to see the two new admissions—the first was an uncomplicated hip replacement admitted for physical therapy. The other was a train wreck.

"Boy, he did a number on himself—concussion, five fractured ribs, fractured pelvis and femur. He'll be here for a good while. I wonder if he'll quit drinking and start using a seat belt. He seems OK, but the wheezing bothers me. His chest X-ray yesterday was normal. He's a long-term smoker, but he hasn't had a cigarette since the accident two weeks ago."

Luke fumbled with the chart, opened it to the medical history, and pointed to one line—allergic asthma since childhood.

87

"That could be it, but he's indoors, and there's not any pollen in the winter," Martin said.

Luke turned to the medication page and pointed.

"Golly, I completely missed that." He turned to Jimmy. "He's on a beta-blocker and an anti-inflammatory. Either could cause an attack of asthma." He deleted the medications and smiled at Luke. "I knew you'd be useful."

Jimmy pulled out the chart for room 125, smiled, and handed it to Martin.

"Oho," Martin said. "Time for your recertification exam, Dr. Brady." He pulled a rubber glove from the cart and waggled his finger. "Think we need another prostate check?"

Luke stepped back and waved his hand.

Martin laughed. "All right, you dodged a bullet today, Dr. Brady."

Luke took the chart from him and pointed to the name. Luke Brady. He tapped his finger on Luke and pointed to himself.

Martin looked puzzled.

Luke repeated the gesture.

"You want me to call you Luke?" he asked.

Luke smiled and nodded.

"OK...Luke." Martin gave a resigned smile. "OK, but it doesn't feel right."

⚬⊰⊹⊱⚬

Luke rearranged the recertification schedule. Instead of getting hammered one day and doing little the next, he saw four or five each day. In the mornings, by the time Martin arrived, Luke had checked all the patients and had their charts ready for review and orders. In the afternoons, he saw the ones to be recertified the following day. The nurses called him anytime they needed help with acute problems. Despite this increased level of activity and his ongoing therapy, the nagging fatigue was gone. Also gone was the insidious boredom of idle time, replaced by the prospect of something new each day.

One new thing was Rachel Graham. Since his stroke, except for Julie, his only female contacts had been restricted to a passing greeting or the ministrations of the therapy or nursing staffs. Rachel's vivacious smile and quick wit made her fun to be around. She was not knock-out gorgeous like Helen. More like extremely attractive, two steps above cute—well-proportioned figure, hazel eyes, and auburn hair done in a pageboy. She reminded Luke of a cheerleader.

Luke hoped it wasn't obvious, but he started arriving at the nurses' station around four thirty each morning. The five or six charts he had to review took twenty minutes at most to organize. This left plenty of time to visit with Rachel before breakfast and make rounds with Martin. Five to six was a slow time on the night shift. Rachel usually had little to do until she checked out to the day crew at six thirty and seemed more than willing to talk with him. She had picked up on his and Jimmy's communication scheme quickly and understood most of what he was trying to say. Obvious or not, he looked forward to their morning sessions.

This morning he found Rachel in the break room.

"Slow night," she said. "Paperwork all done."

He poured himself a cup of coffee and sat down beside her.

"Dr. Brown told me you were his instructor in medical school. I think you're his hero."

Luke smiled.

"I bet you miss teaching."

He nodded.

"Me too. I taught geriatrics at Erlanger Nursing School in Chattanooga."

Why are you here? he mimed.

"Circumstances, sense of obligation, lack of alternatives. My mother has early dementia and is getting more confused. She needs someone to look after her. My brother lives in California with his family. Moving her there would just confuse her more. I don't want her here in Shadydale, and we can't afford anything better. So here I am."

Do you have children?

She looked puzzled. It took several motions and expressions before she understood.

"Do I have children?" she asked.

He nodded.

Her face lit up. "Kate. She's a physical therapist at Erlanger. I saw her almost every day. I miss her. Despite my not-so-subtle prodding, she and Tom haven't presented me with a grandchild yet."

"Mrs. Graham," a nursing assistant interrupted. "Could you help me with Mrs. Baxter?"

Rachel took one last swig of coffee and stood. "Duty calls. See you in the morning."

Several days later, Luke woke with his heart pounding and drenched with sweat. This was just his third nightmare since coming to Shadydale. Totally unexpected, it was one of his most bizarre, but no less frightening. He was in the shower and the fearsome fish lunged out of the drain and grabbed his foot. His leg was halfway down the drain when he woke screaming. Or he thought he was screaming, but Jimmy was still snoring softly. The clock read 2:34. He dressed quietly and walked to the chapel where he sat until 4:00, waiting for the newspaper to be delivered.

"Dr. Brady, would you like some hot chocolate?" Martha called as he passed the open door of her office. Unwilling to cross her, and against his better judgment, he nodded and went in.

She shut the door, cleared some books from the well-stuffed wing chair, and poured two cups of steaming cocoa from a thermos. She sat, tilted back slightly in her desk chair, and smiled faintly at his efforts to avoid the generous display of leg she offered.

"You're up early. Trouble sleeping?"

He nodded.

"Me too. I can never sleep on staff meeting day." She sipped her cocoa. "You know, you and I are a lot alike. You love medicine, and you're really good at it. You probably saved Myrtle's life. The nurses are all pleased having you to call on."

What's going on with her? She's actually being nice. He watched closely. Her pupils were constricted. Her speech was a little too measured, her movements too precise. She was...mellow. She must have had a heavy hit this morning.

She smiled. "From the time I was a little girl, I wanted to be a nurse. I love nursing. And I'm good at it." She motioned to the plaques on the wall behind her desk, leaned forward, and continued in the same placid tone. "There are some ways we're not at all alike. You've always had it easy. Rich daddy. Was he a doctor?"

Luke nodded his head, unwilling to contradict her.

"Whatever. I'm sure money was never a problem for you. Top college. Big man on campus. Easy sailing."

She stood, paced a moment, and leaned against her desk.

"I had to fight and scratch for everything I got. I worked nights as a waitress in a diner to pay for my schooling. But I was smart, and I was determined." Her voice hardened. "And I was pretty, very pretty. I learned about sexual harassment before there was a term for it. My daddy taught me when I was thirteen. He didn't have squat. He was a drunk. A mean drunk. A lecherous drunk. My instructors were no better, always wanting a little something extra to ensure the A I had already earned. At the medical school, the interns and residents, fledgling doctors all, couldn't keep their hands off me. Now I work for that slimy pervert, Crandell. He's just like my daddy. Did you know he has a bed for us in that locked room behind his office?"

Befuddled by this torrent of self-exposure, Luke tried to look as sympathetic as possible. *Why is she doing this?*

She drank the last two swallows of her cocoa. Red blotches dappled her face and neck.

"I was on my way to leaving all that behind," she said in a softer voice, "when you came along. I tried to be friendly with you. Then...then..." Her hands fluttered. "What did I ever do to you?"

She gazed at him a few moments, then returned to her desk and began to shuffle through a pile of paper.

Luke sat unmoving. Martha ignored him. He might as well have been a potted plant. She didn't look up when finally, he rose and left. An hour later she strode to the nurses' station and, disregarding him, decisively began asking questions and snapping orders—nursing supervisor Benson once more.

"Could you brew a fresh pot of coffee?" Rachel asked when he laid his morning charts on the counter. A few minutes later, she poured a cup to the brim and, with a sigh, sank into a chair. "I need this," she said. "The natives were restless last night."

Luke made no move to communicate, letting her unwind in silence. She set her nearly empty cup on the table.

"What's with you and Miss Benson?" she asked.

Luke shrugged, more interested in the whiff of Rachel's perfume than Martha Benson. Chloe, he thought. His favorite. A frequent gift to Helen until she refused to wear it.

"Do you have some history?" Rachel persisted. "She's always making snide remarks about you, but last night she was on a real tear."

Luke waved his hand dismissively.

"She's a brilliant nurse and a great administrator. I don't see how she keeps this place running so smoothly with the limited funds she has."

Luke nodded agreement.

"I can't figure her out. Working nights, I don't have much contact with her. When I do, I find myself walking on eggshells. Everything will be fine until a little something sets her off. She winds up storming to her office. Ten minutes later she's calm, friendly, and helpful, as if nothing happened."

Luke gave a rueful smile. *You don't know the half of it.*

⯈⯇ ⯈⯇

Three weeks later, coffee in hand, Martin strolled to the table where Luke and Jimmy had just finished breakfast.

He slid into a chair. "You won't believe what I did this morning. I slept in. I can't remember the last time I did that." He laid his hand on Luke's arm. "Luke, for the first time since I've been here, I don't feel like I'm constantly treading water to stay afloat. I actually have some time to spend with Judith and the kids. Thank you."

Luke smiled and nodded.

"Think you could handle a little more?"

Luke gave him a quizzical look.

"Dr. Rosman from the medical school has been after me to serve as a preceptor for medical students. I've been putting him off because of my workload."

He smiled. "With you doing all the work, I think I can handle it." He hesitated a moment. "How would you like to help?"

Luke gave him a questioning look.

Martin continued. "They would be here for a two-week rotation. Dr. Rosman specifically wanted you to instruct them in physical diagnosis. They could round with us in the morning and with you in the afternoons after you finish therapy. If they have spare time, they'll come to my office. I've talked to Jimmy about serving as your interpreter when needed."

He paused and looked at Luke. "What do you think?"

Luke's heart raced. He nodded vigorously. "Win! Win!" *Yes. Absolutely. Yes.*

"I thought so," Martin said. "We'll start in three weeks."

After Martin left, they sat digesting what had just transpired.

"We have work to do," Jimmy said at last.

Luke gave him a questioning look.

"I understand you pretty good, but if I'm going to help students know what you mean, I need to understand you better, much better."

Luke motioned for him to continue.

"Give me a day or two. I have an idea."

⚒

Friday evening Jimmy handed Luke a book, *The Clan of the Cave Bear,* by Jean Auel.

"Have you read this?" Jimmy asked.

Luke shook his head.

"It's about Neanderthal cavemen. They couldn't talk, just like you."

Luke nodded.

"They communicated by grunts, noises, hand gestures, and facial expressions."

Luke smiled. He saw where Jimmy was going.

"I was thinking, I bet you...I bet we could do that, too."

Without intent, they had already done this to a degree: shrug with raised eyebrows—"What?"; frown—"I don't think so, I don't like it"; thumbs-up—"OK."

⚒

The next three weeks flew by. They developed new gestures: shrug with eyes widened—"How?"; come here hand motion—"Go on, tell me more"; hands spread, eyes widened—"Anything else?" They added more with each session. Jimmy seemed inherently intuitive.

Luke read his physical diagnosis book twice. He spent two nights highlighting terms for Jimmy to learn, look up in a medical dictionary, or ask Martin if he couldn't get the meaning or pronunciation.

Luke marveled at Jimmy's facility to understand him. At times their communication seemed to flow almost as smoothly as if they were signing.

Sunday night they lolled in their recliners, idly watching a rerun of *The Magnificent Seven.*

Jimmy sighed. "I can't practice anymore."

Luke laughed and nodded agreement.

A knock on the door interrupted their lassitude.

Jimmy opened the door and admitted Debbie. She set down her tote bag, hugged Jimmy, and kissed him on the cheek.

"Uh...Dr. Brady, you know Debbie," Jimmy stammered.

Luke smiled and nodded.

"She's my friend."

Luke struggled not to laugh.

"You guys have worked so hard. The students are coming tomorrow, and you deserve a break," she said.

She took a box of doughnuts, a thermos, three paper plates and some napkins from her tote.

"Here's a little reward."

CHAPTER ELEVEN

Luke sat in the nurses' break room sipping his coffee and fidgeting with his physical diagnosis book. He had slept fitfully and wakened at three.

"Dr. Brady, relax. You know this stuff backward and forward," Rachel said. "You wrote the book, for goodness sake."

Luke smiled and nodded. She was right. He did write the book. He had been teaching it for fifteen years. But he had been able to talk then. Could he teach them anything as a mute? Worse, would he make a complete fool of himself?

"Did you hear about the fellow who went to the doctor complaining he couldn't hear?"

Luke smiled and shook his head. That's Rachel. When all else fails, tell something funny.

"The doctor examined him and said, 'No wonder you can't hear. You have a suppository in your ear.'

"'Well,' the patient said, 'I guess that explains what happened to my hearing aid.'"

When Luke stopped laughing, he stood and picked up his book. Before leaving, he gently squeezed her hand. *Thank you*, he mimed.

━━┊┊┣━

"Morning, Dr. Brady, ready to teach?" Jimmy said, setting down a tray piled high with toast, bacon, and eggs.

Bemused, Luke watched him inhale every crumb.

Jimmy pointed his fork. "You going to eat your bacon and toast?"

Luke smiled and shook his head.

Jimmy slapped the bacon between two pieces of toast and took a large bite, his huge breakfast a distant memory.

Luke idly watched as a few early risers straggled in.

"Here's Dr. Brown," Jimmy said.

Two students in crisp white jackets with stethoscopes draped around their necks trailed Martin.

They look like children playing doctor, Luke thought, then smiled. Just like he'd looked when he was in their place—young, excited, and scared stiff. One of his jacket pockets had bulged from his ophthalmoscope, tuning fork, and percussion hammer; the other strained to hold his fat "poop book," a pocket-size loose-leaf notebook, stretched almost spherical with information for all situations: pediatric medication dosages and IV rates, formulas for correcting metabolic imbalances, pearls of wisdom from his instructors, and myriad other medical factoids, all sorted neatly by alphabetical tabs. These students' jackets hung fashionably, their pockets containing only pencil-sized scopes and smartphones with more data than one hundred poop books, sorted for easy retrieval by Google.

"Dr. Brady, Jimmy, this is Maria Ortega and Steve Calhoun," Martin said.

Luke smiled and shook hands with each of them.

Jimmy gave each a spastic handshake. "Hi, I'm Jimmy."

"Jimmy will be your interpreter. He and Dr. Brady understand each other remarkably well."

"I talk funny, but Dr. Brady can't talk at all," Jimmy said.

Luke and Martin burst out laughing. The students smiled uneasily.

"I've been over the daily routine we worked out," Martin said after they were seated. "They have the handouts from your physical diagnosis course." He turned to the students. "You've learned them thoroughly. Right?"

Yes, sir," they answered in unison.

Before Martin could continue, Luke raised his hand.

He drew a question mark in the air and pointed to his eyes, ears, nose, mouth, and hand.

"You'll find Dr. Brady quite adept at pantomime. He just asked, what are the five senses?"

"Sight, taste, hearing, smell, and touch," Steve said.

Luke drew another question mark, held up four fingers and walked his fingers across the table.

Martin looked at the students. "What did he just ask?"

Blank stares.

He retraced the question mark.

"What?" Maria said.

Martin nodded, looked at Steve, and held up four fingers.

"Four," he said.

He walked his fingers on the table.

They sat silent.

Martin pointed to Jimmy.

"Steps," he said.

Martin fixed the students with his gaze.

No answer.

"What are you here to learn?" Martin asked.

"I've got it," Maria blurted. "What are the four steps of conducting a physical examination?"

"Right," Martin said. "So what are they?"

"Observation, percussion, palpation, and auscultation," they said in unison.

"Good," Martin said. "To quote Dr. Brady, 'Medicine is in a state of constant change—new tests, new tools, new treatments happen daily, but the method of conducting a physical examination never changes—ever.'"

He paused. "Sight: observation—touch: percussion, and palpation—hearing: auscultation. Look, thump, feel, and listen. Every time. In that order. Also, pay attention to any odors. Start taking shortcuts, and the patient loses."

He let them digest this for a moment and went on with a smile. "You usually don't need to taste."

Martin stood. "Dr. Brady realizes there will be times when you don't fully understand him despite Jimmy's able interpretive skills..."

"Impossible!" Jimmy blurted.

"Even so," Martin went on, "if it should happen, jot it down and ask me the next day on rounds. Neither of them will take offense."

He looked at his watch. "Time to start rounds."

After seeing two simple recertifications, he handed a chart to Steve.

"This is Mr. Wilson. He's developed a problem. Talk with him and check him over. Tell us what's wrong when we come back."

Steve swallowed hard. His hand trembled slightly as he took the chart.

They returned forty-five minutes later.

"What do you think?" Martin asked.

"Well..." Steve said, "he has really bad pain in his low back that goes down his right leg and into his foot. It started two days ago. He didn't injure it, and he's never had anything like it before."

Martin nodded. "And what did you find?"

"That's what is so odd," Steve said. "He can walk, bend, and stoop, and the pain isn't any worse. It doesn't hurt when I raise his leg or put stress on his hip joint. His reflexes are normal."

"Anything else?" Martin asked.

"I don't think so," Steve said.

Luke traced another question mark.

"What does he have?" Jimmy asked.

"His symptoms are classic for sciatica, but his examination is normal. I don't know," Steve said.

Luke pointed to his eye.

"What did you see?" Jimmy asked.

An edge of panic crept into Steve's voice. "Just what I said. He can walk, bend, and stoop without his pain changing."

Luke started to Mr. Wilson's room. Jimmy, Martin, Maria, and Steve fell in behind him like little ducklings.

"Hey, Doc," Wilson said to Luke.

Luke smiled, shook his hand, gave a gentle tug to get him to stand, then motioned him to drop his pajamas.

He hesitated and looked at Maria.

"It's OK. She's a doctor," Martin said.

Blushing, Wilson stepped out of his pajamas. A three-inch-wide, swath of red rash started on his lower back, ran across his buttock, down his leg, and onto the outside of his foot.

Luke motioned for them to look closer. Small clusters of blisters cropped up within the rash.

Luke motioned again.

"What is it?" Jimmy asked.

Steve shook his head.

Luke looked at Maria.

"It looks like shingles," she said.

Luke clapped his hands together and smiled at her. He then motioned for Wilson to get dressed.

Martin explained to Wilson what shingles was, how they were going to treat it, and what sort of recovery he could expect.

Back at the nurses' station, Steve said, "I thought shingles only came on the chest."

"It usually does," Martin said. "However, it can occur on any peripheral nerve—on the scalp, face, arm, and..." he smiled at Steve, "on the leg."

⚔

That afternoon, Maria and Steve were still scribbling notes when Luke and Jimmy arrived at the nurses' station.

"Ready to go?" Jimmy asked.

They nodded uncertainly.

Luke took a quarter from his pocket, flipped it, and covered it with his hand. He looked at Maria and raised his eyebrows.

"Tails," she said.

Luke removed his hand. Heads. He handed the chart to her.

Taking a deep breath, Maria began.

"My patient is Mrs. Lucille Willis. She has a long history of rheumatic heart disease."

Chart in hand, she led them to the room and tapped on the door.

"Come on in, honey," Lucille said. "Hi, Dr. Brady. This pretty young doctor is a keeper."

Luke smiled and nodded to Maria.

"Mrs. Willis, is it OK if I show Dr. Brady what I found on your examination?" Maria asked.

With an impish smile, Lucille whipped off her pajama top and flopped back onto the bed.

"Honey, you go right ahead." She pushed a pendulous breast aside. "If these get in the way, just shove them over."

Luke stifled a laugh at Jimmy's reddening face and averted gaze. He gently restrained Maria's hand when she reached for her stethoscope, held up one finger and pointed to his eye.

Maria flinched. "Oh yes. Observation."

She pulled down the sheet and pointed to Lucille's swollen feet. Pressure from her thumb left a deep dent on the top of Lucille's foot.

"She has pitting edema to her knees," Maria said.

Luke nodded and pointed again to his eye.

"See anything else?" Jimmy asked.

"I don't think so," Maria said.

Luke pointed to the distended veins in Lucille's neck.

"I see now," Maria said. "I was so interested in the heart I missed it."

Luke held up three fingers.

"What did you feel?" Jimmy asked.

"Other than the edema, nothing," Maria said.

Luke picked up Lucille's hand and motioned for Maria to take her pulse.

"It's very irregular," she said.

Luke motioned for her to continue.

"Atrial fibrillation?" Maria said.

Luke smiled and gave her thumbs-up, then another three fingers.

"Did you feel anything else?" Jimmy asked.

Maria smiled. "No, but I bet I should have."

Luke laughed and pointed to a spot just below Lucille's left breast. One small area pulsated visibly with each heartbeat. Luke took Maria's hand and gently pressed it over the throbbing spot.

"I feel a vibration, almost like a buzz," Maria said.

Luke nodded vigorously. He then lifted her stethoscope draped around her neck, handed it to her, held up four fingers and pointed to his ear.

"What did you hear?" Jimmy said.

Maria helped Lucille to a sitting position and listened to the back of her chest.

"She has wet crackles in the base of each lung."

"They're called rales," Jimmy said. He gave an embarrassed laugh. "I don't know many of these medical words. Dr. Brady points them out to me in a book and Dr. Martin helps me pronounce them."

Luke nodded his approval and motioned for her to continue.

Maria then listened to Lucille's heart.

"She has a systolic murmur over her mitral valve," Maria said.

Luke pointed to his ear.

"How does it sound?" Jimmy asked.

Maria listened again and thought a few seconds. "Sort of like *swish—swish—swish*," she said.

Luke nodded, raised his eyebrows, and motioned.

"Anything else?" Jimmy asked.

"If she has mitral stenosis, she should have two other sounds—an opening snap and a diastolic rumble, but I don't hear that."

"*Swish*," Luke hissed; "*ta-ta*," he clucked his tongue; "*oooh*," he made a low guttural sound. "*swish, ta-ta, oooh.*"

He motioned.

"Try again," Jimmy said.

Brow furrowed, Maria listened.

"I still don't hear it."

Luke took her stethoscope, tapped on the flat black diaphragm, and pointed up.

Jimmy interpreted. "The diaphragm is for high-pitched sounds."

Luke clicked the diaphragm over, pointed to the cup-shaped metal side, and pointed down.

"The bell is for low-pitched sounds."

Luke handed the stethoscope back and pointed to the small pulsating spot he had shown her earlier.

"*Swish, ta-ta, oooh; swish, ta-ta, oooh,*" he sounded.

Maria placed the bell over the spot, closed her eyes and listened...and listened. Her eyes slowly opened and widened.

"Yes," she whispered. A radiant smile crept over her face. "Oh yes, I hear it. I hear it."

She straightened, removed the stethoscope, and looked at Luke, her face beaming.

"Thank you," she said.

⚔

Every evening after dinner, Luke and Jimmy rehearsed their cases for the following day. Their pantomime and translation got smoother.

Over the next two weeks, Maria and Steve became more thorough and methodical in their examinations. They examined the majority of the patients in Shadydale. Among other things, they learned: five different kinds of heart murmurs; the difference between the dry, crackly breath sounds of pneumonia and the wet, sticky sounds of heart failure; how to detect an enlarged liver or spleen; the sound made by blood rushing through a narrowed artery; the spidery veins that accompanied cirrhosis; and swelling in the neck caused by an enlarged thyroid.

By the end of their rotation, few findings eluded them.

Luke was proud of them, of Jimmy, and of himself.

—≈‖≈—

Two weeks later, Martin was waiting when Luke went for breakfast.

"I got a call from Dr. Rosman last night. He was really excited. Maria and Steve are far ahead of the other students in the usual physical diagnosis curriculum."

Luke smiled.

"He wants to know if you can continue the program. There's a waiting list of students clamoring to come. Are you game?"

Luke nodded vigorously. "Win." *Yes, absolutely, yes.*

—≈‖≈—

Luke wrapped himself in the quiet of the dimly lit chapel. Two hours earlier, the fourth pair of students finished their rotation, thanked him profusely, and left. He and Jimmy now meshed so smoothly that at times, the students didn't seem to notice he couldn't speak. He felt more at ease than at any time since his stroke.

Contentment, happiness—call it what you will—had always been a moving target for him, something just beyond his grasp. Reaching a goal provided momentary satisfaction, which soon gave way to a vague sense of emptiness, a feeling of "Is this all there is?" followed by the search for another goal, another path to happiness. Attending college begat an itch to get on to medical school. Once there, he chafed at the regimented requirements controlled by others. When he got his MD, he'd be his own boss, establish his practice just the way he wanted, and finally be in control. The nearest to contentment he'd ever come was his first ten years in Buxton. Helen was happy. He had a bustling practice. He knew and cared about his patients. In return, they respected and cared about him.

The move to Atlanta and switch to teaching at the medical school cut deep. Helen developed a hard edge, which made home life trying. His knack for diagnosing and teaching brought him attention and provided a rewarding outlet, but didn't provide the desired fulfillment. When he got tenure, he'd be set. But he wasn't. Real happiness and contentment remained a will-o'-the-wisp, something always just beyond his grasp. When he was named dean, he felt he finally had found it. Then the stroke.

Since starting to make rounds and teach, he anticipated each day. He had something to look forward to, a sense of purpose, something that gave his life meaning again, something close to contentment.

Remembering where he was, he smiled and silently gave thanks.

Jimmy flipped his pillow for the sixth time. He had been chasing sleep for four hours. Finally, he threw the covers back, got up, dressed, and made his way to the nurses' station.

"Jimmy, what are you doing up this time of night?" Rachel asked.

"I need to talk to someone."

"Is Dr. Brady asleep?"

"Yes, Mrs. Graham, but I need to talk to someone who can talk back."

"Come back to the break room," Rachel said.

Jimmy fidgeted while she poured two cups of coffee.

"What do you want to talk about?"

Jimmy tensed and bit his lip. "Could you tell me about girls?" The words tumbled out.

"That's a pretty broad subject. Could you be a little more specific?"

"Mrs. Graham, in high school, the girls who were nice seemed to pity me. I never had a date. Since then, I've only been around old women, most of them sick."

"Are we talking about any girl in particular?"

He nodded.

"Debbie?"

He gave a nervous smile and blushed. "Yeah."

"And...?"

Jimmy stared into his coffee. "She's so pretty and smart. How could she like someone like me?"

"What do you mean?"

"Look at me," he blurted. "I talk funny. I walk funny. I look funny."

"You say she's smart," Rachel said.

"Yes."

"Maybe she cares more about what's on the inside—your heart—rather than what's on the outside."

"Easy for you to say. You're pretty, too."

Rachel took a deep breath and tried a different tack. "Has Debbie ever seemed to pity you?"

"I don't think so," Jimmy said.

"Have you ever asked her out?"

"Three times."

"Did she ever turn you down?"

"No."

"Did you have fun?"

His face lit up. "Oh yes."

"Did she?"

"I think so," Jimmy said.

Rachel smiled. "It looks to me as if she already likes you."

"I hope so. If she does, how do I make it last? What do girls want from a guy?"

Rachel gave a brief laugh. "I don't know if I'm the best person to ask that. I married a gorgeous hunk of a man, life of the party, great athlete, talked good, walked good, looked good. It lasted three years. I'd trade all those traits for a man with a good heart."

They sat quietly sipping their coffee.

"You asked what a girl wanted. What might make it last. I'll try to answer you. Be more concerned about her wants, needs, and happiness than yours. Be honest. Never lie. Let her know you appreciate her. Show interest in her, how she feels, and in her hopes, fears, and dreams. Share yours with her. Try to give more than you take."

Jimmy nodded. "That's a lot to think about."

"Sounds simple, but you have to work at it every day," she said.

"Thank you, Mrs. Graham, this really helps," Jimmy said.

Rachel laid her hand on his arm. "Don't worry, Jimmy. You already have most of these qualities. You just have to remember them and practice them."

Back in his room, Jimmy opened his Bible and began to read. *Love is patient; love is kind...*

Luke and Jimmy sat in the rapidly emptying dining room. The clock read 7:17.

"We were supposed to meet at six thirty, weren't we?" Jimmy asked.

Luke nodded.

Another twenty minutes passed.

"There's Dr. Brown," Jimmy said.

Martin slumped into the chair, avoiding eye contact.

"Where are the students?" Jimmy asked.

"There will be no more students," Martin said, his voice tight with anger.

Luke strangled on his coffee. He put his cup down carefully.

"Why?" Jimmy asked.

Martin handed Luke a letter. "It's all in there. She gave me an extra copy and said give it to you." He took a deep breath. "That vindictive bitch, Benson, went to corporate headquarters in Atlanta. She told them patients and their families were complaining the students upset the residents."

"That's not true," Jimmy said. "They asked for the students to see them. They got mad when they didn't."

"I know," Martin said. Another deep breath. "That's not the worst of it. I thought it was just me, but she hates doctors in general." He looked at Luke. "And she hates you in particular. She told them an impaired physician was seeing patients, and it posed a huge malpractice risk." He turned to Luke. "You can't see patients or look at their charts anymore."

Now Luke slumped.

"I've been put on probation. Benson said if you do anything she considers practicing medicine, I'll be fired. You've got to understand. My work at Shadydale funds my practice. My private patients are the poorest of the poor in this county. No one else will see them. Without this job, I'll have to leave. What will happen to them? There was nothing I could do."

For several minutes, no one spoke.

Finally, Martin cleared his throat, "Jimmy do you think you could still help me with the charts on morning rounds? I'd really appreciate it."

"Sure," Jimmy said.

Martin stood. His voice quivered. "Luke...Dr. Brady, I'm sorry. You've done so much for me. I let you down. I am so sorry."

He spun, and head down, strode out.

Luke and Jimmy trudged back toward their room. Martha looked up as they passed the nurses' station.

"Good morning, boys. Staying busy?" she said with a sweet smile and a wink.

Heads down, they kept trudging.

Back in their room they sat in silence. Jimmy opened his Bible but stared out the window.

Luke jumped when he slammed the Bible onto the table.

"I hate her," Jimmy said. "She's the meanest person I've ever known."

Luke did nothing to fuel his anger, but he agreed with his premise.

⟩⟨ ⟩⟨

Luke stared out the window. An unread medical journal lay open on his lap. For the last week, he had left his room only to eat and go to therapy. There was nothing to do. A tap on his door interrupted his idle musing.

"Anybody home?" Rachel called.

He smiled and motioned her to the desk chair.

"Dr. Brady—"

He cut her off with a wave of his hand, then pointed to his name tag on the bedside table.

"OK, Luke. I've missed you."

He shrugged.

"She laid her hand on his arm. " I'm so sorry. I know how much teaching and seeing patients meant to you. I can't understand why Miss Benson did it. Things were going so smoothly."

He nodded.

"I tried talking to her, but that just caused an eruption."

He gave her an "I could have told you so" look.

"I miss our morning visits. If you'll come back, I'll do coffee for the first week."

He motioned agreement.

She stood. "You skipped breakfast three days in a row."

He gave her a surprised look.

"My informants told me." She took his hand and pulled him to his feet. "That ends today. You're taking me to breakfast," she said as they walked hand in hand to the door.

He gave his first sincere smile in days.

She released his hand before entering the hallway.

CHAPTER TWELVE

Each morning, after Jimmy left to help Martin, Luke sat in the deserted dining room, nursing his coffee. Inactivity and lack of order always ate at him. From his college years, each evening he listed what he wanted to accomplish the next day on a legal pad. Helen once said it took a small forest to keep him supplied with paper. He took compulsive pride in checking off each item.

Before now, Luke had never known idle time. From high school until his stroke, his daily routine consisted of work and study. An inactive interlude of more than three or four days, even on holidays or vacation, generated a vague, free-floating uneasiness, alleviated only by resuming his compulsive, busy lifestyle.

When he first arrived at Shadydale, therapy had filled some, but not enough, of his time. After beginning rounding with Martin and then teaching students, he was pleasantly overworked. Benson put an end to that.

He still attended his three hours of therapy each day, but this had devolved into merely going through the motions. Except for mealtimes, the other twenty-one hours were dead time. He resolved not to vegetate. He committed himself to reread *Harrison's Textbook of Medicine* from cover to cover. He forced himself to remain physically active. From his room to the farthest point in Shadydale, the dementia unit, was one hundred sixty-seven steps. It took twenty-two trips to equal approximately one mile. He walked this course twice daily.

Now he wandered in a deep funk, steering clear of Benson and her winks, smirks, and snide remarks. She had vowed to make his life miserable. As much as he hated to admit it, she was succeeding. How could someone so skilled and so bright be so petty?

In his roaming, he found a new hideaway, a bench beyond a broad expanse of lawn beneath the three towering oaks that lent Shadydale its name. The gray February sky matched his mood. The trees were bare except for a few leaves hanging stubbornly against the inevitable end. Just like him. A semicircle of huge boxwoods radiating on either side provided a sense of privacy.

Today he sat bundled against a raw breeze. A steaming cup of tea and four oatmeal cookies he saved from lunch sat on the bench beside him.

"Good afternoon, Dr. Brady."

He spun around at Martha's voice. Unasked, she sat beside him.

"If I didn't know better, I'd think you were avoiding me," she said.

You'd be right, he thought.

"Peace offering." She held a paper plate with three more cookies and another cup of tea. "I know you're upset about not seeing patients. Look at it from my point of view. I'm responsible for everything that happens here. You know how people sue over anything nowadays."

When he made no move to accept her offering, she set it on the bench beside him. "It's really the pits when someone has the power to screw up your life." Her voice hardened. "But you know all about that." She rose and smiled. "There's more to come."

Luke remained seated, weighing her cryptic remark. After finishing his snack, he poured her tea on the ground and left her cookies on the bench for the squirrels.

For the next two weeks, one day blended seamlessly into the next with stultifying sameness. His muscles remained toned, but he sensed the rust and corrosion collecting in his mind and spirit.

The one positive aspect of each day was his early morning visits with Rachel. Her funny stories and small talk got him started. By now, she could read his mimes and expressions almost as well as Jimmy. When Martha wasn't around, she would ask for advice on medical problems that cropped up during the night. He directed her to the appropriate texts or articles. Much of the time, he felt she already knew the answer, but any opportunity to practice or teach medicine helped.

This morning, while waiting for therapy, he sipped his coffee and watched vacantly as the dining room emptied. A balding man with glasses and a faintly familiar face approached his table.

"Dr. Brady, I'm sorry to disturb you, but may I speak with you a moment?"

Delighted with any distraction, Luke motioned him to sit.

"My name is Max Brewer. My mother is Margarete. You've seen her several times."

Luke remembered them both. In contrast to many families, Max visited her two or three times a week. Sometimes he brought two children.

"I'm being transferred to Omaha in three days. I'm her only relative. She has no local friends. It kills me to leave her here alone, but until we're settled, it's impossible to take her with us." He looked away and swallowed hard. Clearing his throat, he faced Luke. "She speaks highly of you. I know it's an imposition, but could you, and maybe Jimmy, visit her from time to time?"

Without hesitation, Luke nodded.

⚊⟨⟩⚊

The next afternoon Luke stood outside room 134 and knocked.

"Come in," Margarete said.

His eyes had to adjust to the dimness. The curtains were drawn, and the lights were off.

"Dr. Brady. Here, sit down. Max told me you might drop by. I didn't expect you so soon."

He motioned to the curtains.

"Yes, open them, please."

Her eyes were red and puffy.

"He's moving, you know."

Luke nodded.

"I know he must go, but it hurts so bad. His visits brighten my whole week. He says they'll come for me as soon as possible, but who knows how long that will be." She clicked on the lamp and took a picture from the bedside table. "That's him with his wife and children," she said, smiling wistfully.

Luke pointed to the two young children. Both had curly blond hair.

Her face lit up. "This is Petey. He's ten. That's Christina. She's eight. And this is Laura, his wife. She's a dear." She gazed at the picture and spoke softly. "Max didn't marry until he was forty-two. He was so busy working and taking care of me. It was just the two of us after Max Sr. died. Max was eighteen." She dabbed her eyes. "I don't know what I'll do without him."

Luke took the picture, gave her a questioning look, and motioned to her small dresser.

"What?"

He repeated the motions.

"More pictures?"

Luke nodded.

"I have a drawer full of them."

Luke motioned to open the drawer.

"You want to see them?"

He smiled and again motioned to the drawer.

She retrieved a picture of a young man and woman.

"That's Max and me soon after we were married," she said, her voice animated.

For the next two hours she conducted a randomly sequenced tour of her life. Finally, she stopped.

"Oh my, I've run on and on."

Luke smiled, squeezed her hand, and stood.

"Thank you so much. Please come again."

<hr />

Clack, clack, clack, clack. Jimmy's quadruple jump left Luke with a single remaining checker. He smiled and threw up his hands. He then pointed to Jimmy and to the door, their agreed-upon sign he needed some time alone in the room. Pointing to himself, then the door, indicated the need for personal time elsewhere.

"See you later," Jimmy said, starting for the door. "Maybe I can find some snacks."

Luke lay back in his recliner with a deep sense of satisfaction. What began as keeping an obligation had morphed into an enjoyable afternoon. And Margarete had gone from crying to smiling.

Suppose he had a patient with crippling arthritis who had pain rated as 10 on a scale of 1 to 10. If he could devise a treatment that reduced it to a level 3, would that not be something worthwhile and meaningful? Of course it would. Just knowing someone cared and understood had lowered Margarete's emotional pain from a level 8 or 9 to a level 2 or 3. Wasn't that equally meaningful? He remembered Tillie. The same thing had happened then.

Ever since Benson had banned him from seeing medical cases, he had struggled to find something that accomplished more than just killing time—something that accomplished something worthwhile. He had prayed for something meaningful in the chapel. Could this be it? Jimmy always worried about the residents who never had visitors. Luke had seen it, too.

Some families remained attentive. They visited and took their loved one on social outings. Some residents had established social contacts with other patients. The majority were alone, a few by choice, most by circumstances. Some had no families. Some families were too far away, too busy, or just didn't care. These residents in particular appeared to be hopeless, resigned to whatever TV had to offer until the undertaker came for them with his black body bag.

Visiting them couldn't hurt. It might even help. There was no way Benson could construe visiting and listening as practicing medicine. Luke chuckled. He couldn't even give advice unless they were involved in some competitive endeavor. Then he could advise them to "win."

Something Father Ryan said in his homily several weeks ago fluttered around the periphery of his consciousness—something about making decisions. He was pretty sure it came from the book of Isaiah. He opened his Bible to Isaiah and began reading, chapter 1, verse 1. He was on chapter 12 when Jimmy returned.

"Want a doughnut?" he asked.

Without looking up, Luke waved him aside and kept reading. Thirty minutes later, he found it. Chapter 30, verse 21.

For Pete's sake, Isaiah, he thought. *Couldn't you have put it in chapter 2?* He read the verse several times. "Whether you turn to the right or the left, your ears will hear a voice behind you say, 'This is the way. Walk in it.'"

That night sleep didn't come. Thoughts of visiting lonely residents dashed and darted through his mind. Suddenly he sensed a voice from the darkness, "This is the way. Walk in it."

⇒⊩⊣⇐

In the early years of their marriage and after their move to Buxton, Helen and Luke's different personality traits bolstered their relationship. He was superorganized with his daily to-do lists. Before leaving on a trip—five days or two weeks, no matter—he knew where they would stay each night and when they would arrive. Even minor changes in familiar routines made him uncomfortable. Rise at six. To bed at ten. Oatmeal for breakfast. Helen had to fight to get him to discard a threadbare sport coat.

If a simple word could describe Helen, it was spontaneous. Spur-of-the-moment trips invigorated her. To Luke's exasperation, she rearranged their furniture at least quarterly. Her spontaneity minimized his rigidity, while his organization moderated her impulsiveness.

After their troubles, the traits that had strengthened their relationship became irritants and wedged them further apart.

Now, Luke was less compulsive, but otherwise had changed little. Convinced he could accomplish something by visiting residents, he methodically developed his plans.

There were 186 total patients, 40 rehab patients whose stays would be short, 122 long-term custodial residents, and 24 residents on the dementia unit. He would begin with the custodial residents. If he saw four a day, he would see them all in a month. Jimmy would follow the same schedule delayed by two weeks, so everyone would be seen twice each month.

Martin still met for breakfast with Luke and Jimmy. He bounced tough cases from here, the hospital, and his office off Luke and kept him abreast of the inner workings of Shadydale. As soon as he finished speech therapy, Luke began his visits.

A familiar aroma struck Luke as soon as he entered the break room. He clapped his hands when he saw the plate of steaming sticky buns on the table. *What's this?* he motioned.

"This is your reward for one month of resident visitation," Rachel said as she poured coffee.

He shrugged dismissively.

"Don't try to blow it off," she said. "You don't realize what a difference you're making. It may not seem like much, but all of the staff—Miss Benson excluded—are talking. The residents are talking. It may seem a little thing, but to some of them, it's the biggest thing in their small world."

She slid a saucer with two sticky buns to him and laid her hand on his arm. "You're my kind of doctor, Luke Brady, my kind of person, my kind of man. You're worth a sticky bun any day," she said with a smile that warmed him more than a sticky bun and coffee ever could.

⇥┼┝⇤

Afternoons were quiet on the long-term resident halls. Most occupants were in their rooms napping, reading, or watching TV. When Luke and Jimmy turned onto Wing Three, a familiar melody greeted them. Drawn by the strains of "Beautiful Dreamer," Luke stood outside the door of room 317. The ID plate read Lily Feingold.

"That's Lily," Jimmy said. "She's—"

Luke hushed him. Her voice was exquisite—light, yet lilting, sounding each note and syllable precisely. He felt a pang of disappointment when the last line, tremulous and full of pathos died… "Beautiful dreamer, awake unto me."

Luke motioned Jimmy to continue. "She sings real pretty. She's crippled. Arthritis. You want to meet her?"

Luke nodded and knocked.

"Come in."

Luke recognized her as the lady who sat at the table nearest the window in the dining room. She was tiny and frail, her back permanently bowed, her hands deformed by rheumatoid arthritis. Yet, bent as she was, there was an air of sophistication in her gaze and bearing.

"Hello, Jimmy. I haven't seen you for a while."

She had a slight European accent Luke couldn't identify.

"Hey, Mrs. Feingold. This is Dr. Brady. He visits people."

"It's good to meet you, Dr. Brady. I've seen you in the dining room."

Luke nodded and gently shook her hand.

"He can't talk," Jimmy said.

"That's what I heard."

"He really liked that song."

"Thank you." She smiled and pointed to a picture on her table. "It was Samuel's favorite. He was a classical musician, but he loved Stephen Foster. He had me sing it every year on our anniversary and his birthday."

Luke studied the picture. They made a striking couple—he in a tuxedo and she in a straight white evening gown.

"We met at Carnegie Hall. Samuel was a cellist, and I had a part in *Madame Butterfly*. I was singing with the Met when the arthritis struck. My singing career ended shortly afterward."

She looked wistfully at her hands, cleared her throat, and said, "I could never convince them it was OK for Aida to have gnarly hands and a crooked back."

Luke sat and motioned her to continue.

"Samuel became the lead cellist in the Atlanta Symphony. I did very well teaching voice. When Samuel died, I was pretty much confined to my wheelchair. We had no children, and our families had been killed during the war. Medical costs had depleted our savings. The daughter of one of the symphony's patrons had been a student of mine. He also owns Shadydale's corporation and arranged for me to live out my days here." She sat quietly. "I'm well fed and cared for, but bored as hell." She pointed to a stack of books on her bedside table. "That helps me maintain my sanity. The Buxton librarian brings me two or three new selections every two weeks."

Luke examined them—two fiction and one nonfiction, all recent best sellers—a giant leap from the *Reader's Digest*s and battered inspirational volumes on the library shelf in the dining room. He pointed to them and to himself.

"I'm sorry, I don't understand," Lily said.

"He wants to know if he can read them after you're finished," Jimmy said.

"Of course," she said. "I'd love to discuss them with you." She caught herself. "I'm so sorry."

Luke waved the apology aside, pointed to her, then the books, then himself, then his ear."

"He says he'd like to hear what you have to say about them," Jimmy said.

"I'd love that," Lily said, her eyes shining. She handed him one dealing with Israel and the Middle East. "This is very thought provoking."

He nodded his thanks.

Her eyes sparkled, and she flashed a mischievous smile. "Come back when you've finished. I'll tell you what you should think."

⟞⟢ ⟣⟝

Word of his visits spread. Everyone was eager to see him. Most showed him pictures and talked about their families. Rachel and

Amy began a collection, and with Father Ryan's help, they purchased inexpensive photo albums for Luke to help organize on subsequent visits. Many shared their problems and heartaches. Every day there were surprises.

Gertrude was ninety-two and had been a housekeeper for Franklin Roosevelt at Warm Springs. She loved Eleanor, tolerated Franklin—he was too high-class—but wanted no part of "that hussy, Lucy Mercer."

Buddy, one of the wheezer geezers, had been a state representative until they outlawed the poll tax. "Then the blacks booted me out."

Johanna taught elementary school children for sixty-two years, the first eighteen in a one-room schoolhouse.

Livingston's grandfather had been a slave. He shined shoes in the Atlanta train station until he joined the army right after Pearl Harbor. He drove trucks across Europe with the Red Ball Express, then big rigs for forty years after his return.

Luke vacillated between admiration and despair. These and many other residents were a microcosm of disappearing rural America. Most had lived useful, productive lives as farmers, factory workers, teachers, carpenters, painters, plumbers, and merchants selling groceries, dry goods, and farming supplies. Two or three families lived together or within a stone's throw of each other.

Then the interstate bypassed Buxton, family farms couldn't compete with agricultural conglomerates, and factories moved to the third world. Their children departed for cities with more job opportunities and amenities. Many parents were left to grow old in a withering backwater and eventually to be warehoused in places like Shadydale until they died, often alone.

He shuddered. If not for Julie and Jimmy, he was no different.

Luke sat on the edge of his bed and stretched. Five forty-five. He woke later than usual. Jimmy was up and gone.

"Wake-up snack." Jimmy lurched in, carrying a tray with two cups of coffee and three doughnuts. "These were left over from the night shift, and they said we could have them."

He put a dripping cup on Luke's table.

"I tried to rush and sloshed some of your coffee. Sorry."

Jimmy scarfed down his doughnut and broke the other in half. Luke shook his head at his proffered share.

"Isn't this cozy?" Martha's voice interrupted the slurp of their coffee. "The Bobbsey twins."

She stood beside the TV table.

"You think you're so smart." She pointed at Luke. "I told you I'd get even. You ruined my life. Now, bit by bit, I'm going to ruin yours. You can't be a doctor anymore. There's more. It starts now. No more therapy. We both know you're never going to get better. But as long as you go to therapy, there's always a shred of hope. That's over. Gone. Kaput. I'm telling Helen and Julie today."

They sat staring at her.

"Oh, Julie will whine, but Helen won't do anything. We're good friends now. She agrees with me. I don't know which of us hates you the most. You're not leaving here until she says you can. Knowing her, that's not likely. Even if she changes her mind, I'll never let it happen.

"And you." She pointed at Jimmy. "You can kiss your snacks goodbye. I told the dietary workers and the staff I'd fire anyone giving you food other than at mealtime."

"You can't do that!" Jimmy blurted.

"Shut up, you spastic retard. I can, and I will. The queen bee can do anything she likes."

She laughed at Jimmy's stunned expression.

"Yes, I know about your little nicknames. I know everything that goes on around here. Even your kissy-kiss meetings in the chapel with Watson. You can scratch those, too. She's going on night shift."

"But how will she finish her nursing school?" Jimmy said.

"Not my problem. You should've thought about that before teaming up with him," she said, pointing at Luke.

She turned when she reached the door.

"Enjoy your doughnuts," she said and winked.

"Come in," Martha said to Helen and Julie. She motioned to Dan Crandell, Dr. Brown, and the occupational, physical, and speech therapists. "I think you've met everyone."

Helen and Julie took their seats at the large conference table. Martha remained standing.

"Just to bring you up to date. Insurance requires that we evaluate patients receiving skilled care every thirty days to see if they still qualify for skilled physical therapy. When they have progressed as far as their conditions allow, they are removed from skilled therapy."

Julie interrupted, "What—"

"Let me finish," Martha said, cutting her off. She motioned to the others. "We've met, and we all agree Dr. Brady will have no more significant improvement."

"What does that mean?" Julie asked, her voice skeptical.

"As I explained to Mrs. Brady, his insurance will no longer cover the cost of any further rehabilitation or therapy expenses."

"You mean he will get no more therapy?" Julie asked.

"Not unless the family pays for it."

"How much would it cost?"

"His insurance will cover his custodial care. To continue re-hab and therapy requires approximately twelve hundred dollars a month. This will not be covered by insurance," Martha said.

"That's completely out of the question," Helen snapped.

"But, Mother, he's trying so hard. I think he's still improving. Don't you agree, Dr. Brown?" Julie said.

Martin stared at the papers before him, refusing to make eye contact, and shrugged.

"People see what they want to see," Martha said.

"Dr. Brown, don't you think he can get better?" Julie persisted, near desperation.

Martin's eyes pleaded with her. "He does work hard, and he has made remarkable progress. With his cane, he walks with just the slightest limp."

"See," Julie spoke directly to Martha.

"But," Martin continued, "his walking has not improved significantly in the last six weeks. His right hand is the same as three months ago, and his speech is no better than right after his stroke. I'm afraid he's about as good as he's ever going to be."

"But he could get better?" Julie asked.

Martin sighed and waggled his hand. "Perhaps."

"Quit beating around the bush," Martha snapped, her face flushing. "Yes or no, do you think he will improve at all?"

Martin seemed to shrink. "No," he whispered.

"Then it's settled. After this week, Dr. Brady will no longer be skilled."

"Mother..." Julie pleaded, teary-eyed.

"You heard the doctor," Helen said.

Julie dabbed her eyes as everyone filed out. Martin was the last to leave.

"I'm really sorry, Mrs. Vaccaro, but there's really nothing I can do," he said.

Unconvinced, Julie replied, "I guess not," and walked out.

Martha and Helen were talking in the hall.

"I want to see Daddy before we go," Julie said.

"You go ahead. Miss Benson and I need to discuss some things," Helen said.

"Do you want me to wait for you in his room?"

"No, I don't have time to see him today. I'll meet you in the lobby."

Julie walked away. *I'm sure you don't want to face him after what you're doing to him. I wish I could do more.*

⟫⟪

Luke broke into a huge smile, stood, and held out his arms when Julie entered the room. She ran across the room and flung her arms around him, struggling not to cry.

"Daddy, they're stopping your therapy."

He tapped his chest, then his head.

"Win." *I know.*

"You already know?" Julie asked.

He nodded.

"You'll keep working on your own, won't you?"

He laughed, gave her a thumbs-up, and motioned to the chair.

She sat down. "My girls have won two games in the playoffs. We're playing Midland this Friday. They will probably clobber us, but it's been a good year." She rattled on about school, Mark, and her pregnancy—anything to avoid the reason for today's visit. Finally, she rose to go.

"I love you, Daddy. I'm going to work on Mother. Maybe we can still get you back nearer Atlanta."

⟫⟪

Luke sat in the courtyard and tossed another handful of crumbs from the sack of stale bread. Four pigeons and a swarm of sparrows picked and pecked, pausing only when a boisterous blue jay scattered them.

"Dr. Brady, could I speak with you a moment?" Donna Henderson asked as she approached.

He nodded and patted the bench.

"Amy told me you weren't going to therapy anymore and had time to visit more residents. She's really excited. Says they love it."

Luke shrugged and smiled.

"My patients on the dementia unit almost never have visitors. Could you stop in sometime? It might help."

After a few moments of thought, he nodded.

"Around ten is the best time. They've dressed and eaten by then. They get tired and grumpy as the day goes on." She stood and grasped his hand. "Thank you."

He continued idly strewing crumbs. It might help, or it might just agitate them more. Most of the residents ached to have someone really listen to them. But what if they had nothing to say? Or what they said was incoherent? He hectored medical students to always abide by the principle, *primum non nocere,* first do no harm. What if his visits did more harm than good?

⇥⇤

The dementia unit consisted of a long hallway with rooms on either side. As he walked to the nurses' station midway down the hall, a few residents were still in bed. Others sat in trayed chairs lined along the wall; others shuffled about aimlessly. Each wore nearly identical outfits: blue or green wraparound open-down-the-back gowns on the women and scrubs on the men. Their names were stenciled at the neckline. Many wrapped themselves in blue chenille bathrobes. All wore cloth, rubber-soled slippers. Women outnumbered men about six to one.

"Thank you for coming," Donna said. She pointed to a large room where two residents stared in the vicinity of a TV. "That's the activity room. Those who can't go to the main dining room get their meals there."

A tall, angular woman carrying a worn Raggedy Ann doll tugged at Donna's arm. A large port-wine stain, furrowed by a frown, covered her left eye and forehead.

"Dr. Brady, I'd like you to meet Sally."

Luke shook her hand. She stared at him for a moment, then looked away.

"She was the charge nurse in the newborn nursery at Buxton for years," Donna said.

Luke recognized her now. She had cared for many of his deliveries. Those babies had been her life.

He took the stethoscope from Donna's pocket and put the buds in his ears. With a questioning look he pointed to Sally's doll. Retaining her grip, she eased the doll toward him. Her eyes brightened as he somberly listened to its chest and felt its stomach. He patted it, smiled, and pushed it back to her. She kissed it; then clutching it to her breast, she walked away smiling.

"I think that's the first time I've ever seen her smile," Donna said. "I have to pass meds, but I want you to see one other person before I go."

She led him to a portly man who sat quietly, hands folded on his desktop chair. He had what the medical students called the "thousand-yard stare."

"Dr. Adams, this is Dr. Brady. You worked with him several years ago in Buxton."

Dr. Adams had been the only internist in Buxton. Luke had consulted him often.

When Luke shook his hand, the doctor's unfocused stare seemed to pass right through him. Retrieving a chair and a stethoscope from the nurses' station, Luke sat beside him. He took Dr.

Adams's fingers and placed them over his wrist. Feeling a pulse, a brief flicker of recognition crossed his face, and then he resumed staring. Luke placed the stethoscope in Dr. Adams's ears and held it to his chest. He listened briefly. A glimmer of what seemed to be recollection again flitted across his face before he returned to staring. As Luke started to remove the stethoscope, Dr. Adams grasped it. Luke smiled, nodded, and left it in place. For the rest of his visit, from time to time he saw Dr. Adams feel his own pulse, then listen to his heart for a few seconds.

Because of the residents' short attention spans, visits in the unit were briefer than on the residential floors. Luke saw over half of them before lunch.

"Thank you for coming," Donna said as he was leaving. "You may not see it now, but it helped."

On his way to the door, Sally smiled and waved.

He sat on the bench beneath the oaks, reviewing what had happened. Some patients seemed totally lost and unreachable. But for many, small gestures seemed to bring a brief peace, maybe even pleasure—not much—but more than was there before. What intrigued him most was the brief flicker of recognition, perhaps even memory, he saw in Sally's and Dr. Adams's eyes when reintroduced to familiar past activities or in others when they examined photos of their families or scenes from their past. Almost as if in the deep recesses of their minds, these triggered a memory that stirred and set out on a neural pathway to consciousness. On rare occasions, the memory reached its destination and sparked a momentary flash of remembrance. Sadly, more often than not, faulty synapses shunted the memory onto side roads where it ground to a halt in a tangle of dead nerve fibers, leaving only blank stares.

Luke gave a rueful laugh. He wasn't much different. Words, like their memory, were there, not buried, but in his case ready for release. He sent them speeding down a fast track to his tongue and vocal cords only to have them plunge into the black abyss of his stroke, never to emerge.

———

"Dr. Brady, I don't like to go there. It makes me sad," Jimmy said. "Besides, I look funny. I talk funny. It scares a lot of them."

Luke held up one finger.

"OK, just this once."

Jimmy, eyes fixed firmly on the floor at his feet, accompanied Luke into the unit and on to Donna's office.

"You going to let me in on the big secret?" she asked.

Jimmy gave a short laugh. "Dr. Brady brought me to interpret," he said. "He wants to do two things."

"OK," Donna said. "What?"

"Dr. Brady tried to tell me, but I couldn't understand. Something about when the people here get restless and grumpy."

"Midafternoon," Donna said.

Jimmy nodded. "Lily Feingold on Wing Three sings real pretty. Dr. Brady thought it might help calm your patients if she sang to them."

"At times, music does seem to pacify some of them," Donna said. "It couldn't be too loud or lively."

"You can tell her what type of music you want," Jimmy said. "She says she doesn't need a piano. She said it would be nice to have an audience again."

"I'll talk with her," Donna said. "What's the other thing?"

"Dr. Brady had me talk with Father Ryan. He has five women from his church who want to help," Jimmy said.

"Go on."

Jimmy explained Luke's proposal.

"That sounds wonderful," Donna said. "I'll have to get Miss Benson's approval. When I tell her Dr. Brady suggested it, I'm sure she'll agree."

Jimmy and Luke both shook their heads vigorously.

"No, no!" Jimmy said. "She doesn't like Dr. Brady. Tell her it's your idea, and Dr. Brady doesn't think much of it."

"You sure?" Donna said.

Both nodded. "We're sure," Jimmy said.

Three days later, five ladies set up shop in the activities room, makeup kits and nail polish at the ready.

They helped each female patient select colors for manicures, combed their hair, and applied lipstick, blush, and eye shadow.

"I can't believe it," Donna said, watching as each one examined herself in the full-length mirror set up by the nurses' station. "They're absolutely radiant."

When the room emptied, one of the church ladies approached Donna.

"Are there any others?" she asked.

Nine more," Donna said," but they're too far gone to understand."

"We'll see. Take us to them."

"Thank you so much," Donna said when they had finished.

"No, thank you. We'd like to come every Tuesday, if that's OK."

Two days later, Luke wheeled Lily onto the dementia unit. Donna met them with a harried expression. Patients milled about, screams came from one room, sobs filtered from another.

"Tough audience," Lily said with a wry smile.

Luke and Donna burst out laughing.

Donna led them to the activities room. Sally and another woman wandered out, but an aide herded them back in. Twelve other residents sat in trayed chairs or shuffled around. Donna placed

Lily in the center of the entrance. She and Luke stood on either side, hindering escape.

"Showtime," Lily said and began softly singing, "Beautiful dreamer..." By the time she finished, all shuffling had stopped. Without hesitation, she slid into "Sweet Hour of Prayer." One or two women sang along with her.

Amazing, Luke thought, as the flicker of recognition he had noticed before lit a face for a moment and faded, then flitted to another and another like so many fireflies. After Brahms's "Lullaby," Lily segued into "Jesus Loves the Little Children." Several of the residents joined her and sang as much as came to mind. Sally hugged Raggedy Ann to her breast and stroked her hair throughout Lily's finale. Dr. Adams's distant stare never wavered, but when the song ended, he clapped three times.

"I can't believe what I just saw," Donna said. "Thank you so much, Mrs. Feingold."

Lily gave a slight curtsy. "Call me Lily. I shall come each Thursday afternoon."

"Please do," Donna said.

Lily gave Luke a mischievous smile. "Home, James."

CHAPTER THIRTEEN

"Mother, you don't need to do this," Julie said as they pulled into Shadydale's parking lot.

"The attorneys say I do," Helen replied.

"But you already have control of all the finances."

"We've been over this," Helen said. "It's not legal until Luke assigns me power of attorney for his financial affairs."

"If he can practice medicine, he can manage his money," Julie said. "Ask Dr. Brown. He'll tell you."

Helen parked and switched off the engine. "Dr. Brown won't do anything. He wants to keep his job. Besides, I have two neurologists who will say otherwise." She heaved an impatient sigh. "He can't talk. He can't write. How's he going to give directions to brokers, bankers, and insurance people? By pantomime? Is Jimmy going to interpret his wishes?"

"If he can't write, how can he sign the agreement?" Julie asked.

"And why can't he write?" Helen asked.

"Well...you know...The stroke locked that away in his brain."

Helen pounced. "Exactly, who knows what else is locked away—or what will be locked away next week or next month. I can't take that risk."

"But he still can't sign."

"I talked with the occupational therapist. She said he can copy his signature. My attorney says that's all we need."

"But—"

"Julie, stop it! I let you come with me because you insisted you explain it to him."

Julie said nothing.

Helen opened her door. "Come on, let's get this over with."

⇥⊢⊣⇤

Luke's expression grew incredulous as Julie told him the situation. He spread his hands.

"Why?" Julie said. "Who knows? But you know when Mother gets something in her head, she's like a dog with a bone. No matter how unnecessary, inconvenient, or hurtful, she won't let go until she gets her way."

Luke nodded, but instead of his usual tolerant resignation when dealing with Helen, his gaze hardened, and his jaw clenched. He grabbed his cane, took a book from the table, and started toward the door.

In the conference room, Helen, Martha, Dan Crandell, and Wilma sat at the long table. Luke helped Julie to a seat opposite them. He sat directly across from Helen and fixed her with a gaze that could freeze water.

"Good afternoon, Luke," she said.

He didn't respond.

She cleared her throat. "Did Julie explain why we're here?"

Still no response. Helen looked at Julie.

"He understands," Julie said.

134

The silence was deafening.

"OK then," Helen said, her voice regaining its usual forceful-ness. "Let's get on with it." She pushed a two-page legal document toward him. "Do you want to read it?"

"He read the copy you gave me," Julie said.

"Good," Helen said. "All you need to do is sign it." She pulled a larger document from her briefcase. "Here's a copy of your will. You can copy your signature from it."

He took the power of attorney and flipped the will back at her. He opened an autographed copy of *Basics of Physical Diagnosis*. With painstaking effort, he copied a shaky replica of his signature then slid the document back to her.

She handed it to Martha. "Miss Benson and Mr. Crandell will witness it, and Wilma will notarize it."

All five jumped, and Wilma gave a spontaneous yelp when Luke slammed his hands on the table and lurched to his feet.

"What is it?" Helen stammered.

He pointed at Martha and shook his head violently.

"I don't understand," Helen said.

Luke snatched the document. He pointed at Martha then the paper, wagged his finger, and shook his head. He jerked it away when Helen reached for it. With deliberate slowness he pointed at Martha, mimed signing the document, then held it up as if to tear it in two.

"You don't want Miss Benson to be a witness?" Helen asked.

He made a look of mock surprise and gave her thumbs-up.

"Quit being foolish, Dr. Brady," Martha said. "You must have two witnesses."

Luke again shook his head and pointed at Martha. He laid the paper in front of Julie and pointed at her.

"You want me to sign it?" Julie asked.

He smiled at her and nodded. Julie hesitated a moment, then picked up the pen. Before she could sign, he laid his hand on her arm. He pointed at Martha and then at the door. She glared back defiantly.

"I'm sorry, Miss Benson, but we need to get this done. Could you please leave?" Helen said.

Martha didn't budge.

"Just go, Benson," Crandell said. "Let's get this over with."

Red-faced, she fixed Luke with a glare that would peel paint.

Just before she stormed out, he smiled at her and winked.

═══╬═╬═══

They drove in silence for fifteen minutes.

"That was very melodramatic," Helen said. "I really felt sorry for Miss Benson. There was no reason for him to embarrass her."

"Embarrass her!" Julie yelled. "You drive all the way down here to humiliate Daddy, and you worry about Benson? You know she does everything she can to make Daddy miserable."

"I didn't come to humiliate Luke. It was something that had to be done."

"Why didn't you let me bring him to Atlanta and do it quietly in the attorney's office like I asked?"

Helen didn't answer.

"Is money really that important to you?"

Helen's voice rose half an octave. "You're damn right it is. You've never been poor. Well, I have. My father was a farmer, a poor farmer. We barely had enough to eat. I worked two jobs to put your father through school. We had nothing. I will never be poor again."

"And you're not. Daddy provided well for us."

"So now I'm supposed to sacrifice for Mr. Wonderful all over again?"

Julie struggled for control.

"You really hate him, don't you?"

"No, I don't hate him, although I have good reason to," Helen said, as much to herself as to Julie.

"What reason?" Julie could hold it no longer. "He's always been kind and considerate. I've never even heard him raise his voice to you. But I've never seen you show him any affection."

Julie gave an involuntary scream as Helen stomped on the brakes and came to a skidding halt on the shoulder of the road.

Helen turned toward her, eyes blazing. Her lips were drawn tight, almost in a sneer.

"I will not be the villain here. I will not."

"What do you mean?"

"You've always been Daddy's girl. You worshiped him. You tolerated me."

"That's not true."

"The hell it's not. I did the best I could. If that wasn't enough, the fault is his, not mine."

"What are you talking about?"

Helen took long, hard breaths and clenched the steering wheel so tightly her knuckles turned white.

"Tell me," Julie said, her voice determined.

After more deep breaths, Helen slumped back, her gaze fixed somewhere far down the highway. When she began to speak, her voice was a flat monotone.

"He made me promise not to tell you, but I think it's time. I had a horrible pregnancy with you. I nearly died. I was so sick they sent me to Atlanta to be near the specialists. I stayed with my mother when I wasn't in the hospital. Luke said he couldn't leave his practice unattended, so he stayed in Buxton."

She clenched and unclenched her grip on the wheel.

"Oh, he came to see me on weekends—when he didn't have call or pressing medical matters, of course. Just like always, medicine before me."

Her voice began to rise.

"But during the week, while I'm struggling to keep us alive, what was he doing?"

She glared, chin quivering at Julie.

"What?"

Her voice took on a wailing, keening quality.

"He was banging the blond slut who worked in his office."

She collapsed on the steering wheel, her body jerked with deep, wrenching sobs.

Julie sat, mute.

Helen gradually calmed, dabbed her tears with a tissue, and blew her nose. She looked at Julie's stunned, wide-eyed gaze and began to laugh.

"That's right. Your heroic knight's armor is all tarnished. He's just a common, whoring lecher like all the rest. So, yes, I guess I hate him. And I'm not sorry he's sick. Now he knows what it is to be helpless and alone."

"I don't believe you," Julie said.

"Believe it."

"Daddy would never do something like that."

Helen fixed her with a long stare.

"Why don't you ask your daddy?

CHAPTER FOURTEEN

J immy looked up from the chessboard. "Julie," he said and clambered to his feet.

Beaming, Luke stood and stretched his arms to Julie.

She ignored his gesture. "Jimmy, would you excuse us?" she said.

"Uh, sure, Julie," he stammered and shuffled out, casting a puzzled look over his shoulder.

Julie avoided Luke's proffered hug and sat in the empty chair across the table from him. "Please sit down, Daddy. We need to talk."

His smile gone, Luke sat.

Julie fumbled with the strap of her purse. "Daddy..." She hesitated. "Daddy, Mother told me you cheated on her; you had an affair while she was pregnant with me. I know that can't be true."

Luke's head snapped back as if he had been slapped. His stomach flipped, and a spreading nausea enveloped him.

"It isn't true, is it?"

He sat unmoving, his gaze fixed on his hands folded in his lap.

"Is it true, Daddy?" Her voice rose in pitch and volume. "Is it?"
Head still downcast, he slowly nodded.

"Daddy, how could you? Why? Why?"

His eyes pleaded with her. "Win." *You don't understand. I was so sad. So lonely. I'm sorry.*

She slumped back and stared at the ceiling, chin quivering, fists clenching and unclenching. Her silence screamed at him. Her chair clattered over when she finally stood. He squirmed as she skewered him with a glare that, to him, brimmed with combined fury, hurt, and disappointment.

"Win." *Julie, please, I'm so sorry.*

"Take your 'win' and shove it, Daddy. Goodbye."

Panicky, he called after her, emitting a mixture of "wins" and guttural noises, but she was gone.

⊫⊰⊱⊪

Jimmy sat at the table, nervously shredding a napkin. His breakfast sat untouched before him. Martin pulled out a chair and sat down. "Where's Luke?" he asked.

"Dr. Brown, something's wrong, bad wrong. You need to see him," Jimmy said.

"What's the matter?"

"Julie came to see him Saturday. She seemed mad. I think they had a fight. Dr. Brady was crying after she left. Now he won't get out of the room. He barely gets out of bed. He won't eat. He just sits and stares."

Martin headed for Luke's room.

⊫⊰⊱⊪

Luke, unshaven and still in his pajamas, sat staring out the window.

"Hey, Luke, I missed you at breakfast. I have three really tough cases I need to run by you," Martin said.

140

Luke slowly shook his head.

"What's the problem, Luke?" Martin persisted.

No response.

"Is something wrong with Julie? Something about the baby?"

"Win." *Go away and leave me alone.*

"Come on, Dr. Brady, let us help you."

Luke turned and faced them. His entire bearing radiated a deep sadness. Luke pointed toward the door—once, twice, three times.

"I'll come back later," Martin said.

Luke shrugged and turned back to the window, alone with his thoughts. *Luke, you worthless piece of shit. What will Rachel think when she finds out? That façade you so carefully built is crashing down. You blunder around, screwing up people's lives. First you destroyed Helen. You cost Jimmy most of the small pleasures that made his life livable. You made Debbie's nursing school doubly difficult.* His throat tightened. *And now Julie.*

After rounds, Martin returned as promised. Luke didn't turn from the window.

"Luke, I don't know what happened, but you seem terribly depressed. I'd like to start you on an antidepressant. Is that OK with you?"

Luke replied with a noncommittal shrug.

"You know it'll take a while to take effect. As soon as you're better, I could really use your advice on several cases."

No response.

"I'll see you tomorrow," Martin said.

Less than an hour later, Martha walked in with two pills in a plastic cup. She smiled and winked at him.

"Feeling a little low?" she asked. "Too bad." She poured a cup of water. "Here you go." She winked again. "A pill can solve a lot of problems. Take it from a pro."

He put the pills on his tongue. While reaching for the water, he maneuvered them between his cheek and gum and made a show of throwing down a large swig of water.

She patted him on the shoulder. "That's a good boy."

As soon as she left, he went to the bathroom, shut the door, and spit them into the toilet.

━━◄┼┼►━━

Luke had been this low only once before in his life. Then, he had been young, healthy, and diverted by more work than he could possibly handle. He possessed some hope for the future. Busyness and fatigue provided enough distraction to tide him over until his mental status stabilized. Now he was no longer young or healthy. He had nothing of any significance to do. And he was hopeless.

He stopped his visiting and had Jimmy inform the nurses he wouldn't be back. Jimmy began visiting after rounds in addition to the afternoon. Rather than two visits a month, the residents would receive one from Jimmy, but that was better than nothing.

Luke withdrew to his room. He spent the majority of his time sitting in his chair, staring out the window. Basic hygiene deteriorated: pajamas unchanged, hair uncombed, shaving ignored. He did brush his teeth. His only nutrition was sandwiches, fruit, and cartons of juice and milk Debbie spirited from the kitchen during the night before Martha arrived. These would have remained untouched except Jimmy cajoled and threatened him until he ate.

━━◄┼┼►━━

"Luke."

He cringed at the sound of Rachel's voice and burrowed deeper under the covers, pretending to be asleep. *Go away, Rachel, just go away.*

"Don't ignore me, Luke Brady," she snapped. "I know you're awake."

He threw the covers back and sat up.

"My God, you look awful," she blurted.

Thanks, that really helps.

"I'm sorry," Rachel said. "Jimmy told me some of what's going on. I've been worried sick."

He shrugged and avoided eye contact.

"I don't want to intrude—"

He cut her off with an impatient wave of his hand. *Then don't intrude.*

She clenched her jaw and plowed on. "Dr. Brown said you were very depressed. Let me help."

He motioned for her to leave.

"Luke, you mean a lot to me. It breaks my heart to see you so sad. Maybe I could—"

"Win!" he shouted. *You can't help me. Nobody can. Now go away before I screw up your life, too.*

She cringed at his uncharacteristic anger. "I don't know what you just said, but I know you don't mean it."

He jabbed his finger toward the door.

Her hand trembled as she laid it on his arm. "Whenever you want me back, I'll be right there," she said. Then she left.

⇥⊹⇤

The nightmares returned, more menacing than ever. At first, each had the same pattern as before—a fleeting cinema-like review of disjointed, vaguely familiar scenes, climaxed by the fish with fearsome teeth and eyes leaping from a body of water—a pond, a river, a fountain, a bathtub, even a large glass of water—and dragging him flailing beneath the surface. He would wake, heart pounding, drenched with sweat. Sometimes he screamed loud enough to wake Jimmy.

After two nearly sleepless weeks, the pattern changed. The review of past scenes gave way to something more ominous: a dark room with an open casket too high for him to see into, a cemetery on a moonless night, but what followed was less frightening. Instead of attacking him, the fish lolled with its head protruding from the water. The evil red eyes still glowed, and a sardonic smile exposed the jagged teeth. Each night it bobbed a bit closer, moving its head as if beckoning him. Tonight the hypnotic eyes gazed at him from the water's edge, and he threw his arms around it. As they plunged beneath the surface, in place of his former terror, he felt a warm sense of relief.

He woke and smiled. He knew what he had to do.

CHAPTER FIFTEEN

He rose early, showered, shaved, and put on clean clothes. He made his bed, then spent the day cleaning and straightening the room. When an encouraged Jimmy tried to talk with him, he motioned he wanted to be alone.

Late that night, Jimmy leaned on the counter where Rachel was charting. She glanced at the clock.

"You're up awfully late, Jimmy. It's after midnight."

He shrugged.

"Are you feeling bad?"

He shook his head.

She smiled and touched his hand.

"Come on. Maybe I can perk you up."

She led him into the nurses' lounge. A larger platter of chocolate chip cookies sat on the table. She poured two cups of hot chocolate and handed him one.

"Have a cookie," she said.

He sipped the cocoa and nibbled on a cookie.

"What's the matter, Jimmy?"

He laid the cookie down and took a deep breath.

"It's Dr. Brady. He's so sad since Julie doesn't come to see him anymore."

Rachel nodded. "I know. He won't see me. Maybe I should say something to Dr. Brown."

"No, don't, please. They'll just dope him up more or send him away."

She nodded but said nothing.

He took another bite. His face lit up with a smile.

"Miss Benson won't let me get snacks anymore. Some hot chocolate and cookies might cheer him up."

"It just might," she said.

She loaded a stack of cookies on a saucer, heated them in the microwave and placed them on a tray along with another cup of steaming hot chocolate. She handed the tray to Jimmy and put her finger to her lips. "Not a word about this to anyone."

He blinked several times. "Thank you, Mrs. Graham. It'll be our secret."

Jimmy paused at the door and steadied the tray. Luke sat at his table, staring out the rain-soaked window into the darkness, split from time to time by a jagged streak of lightning.

Jimmy pasted on a large smile. "Ta-da! Look what I've got."

Luke watched as Jimmy pulled his chair over, moved the book and set a cup of hot chocolate and the stack of cookies on the table. Taking one for himself, Jimmy took a large bite.

"Umm," he said. "They're still warm; eat up. Mrs. Graham said we have to destroy all the evidence."

Luke watched him eat. *Jimmy, you sweet, innocent anomaly. You got crapped on by life—no parents, a twisted, spastic joke of a body, little future outside of Shadydale—yet you live and enjoy life one moment at a time. I can't recall you ever complaining. How do you do it?*

Luke motioned for him to come closer. Jimmy clumped his chair nearer. Clumsily, he drew Jimmy to him and kissed him softly on the forehead. When he released his grasp, Jimmy slid his chair back, avoiding eye contact.

"Don't let them get cold," he blurted, focusing new attention to his cookie.

Luke made a show of scarfing down his cookies and sipping his cocoa. Saucer and cup empty, he rose, rubbed his stomach, and gave Jimmy a hearty smile. Taking a clean pair of pajamas, he disappeared into the toilet and showered.

"Dr. Brady, you look like your old self," Jimmy said when Luke emerged, clean, shaved, and well groomed.

Luke smiled and made a big show of stretching and yawning. Then he turned his lamp off and crawled into bed.

Luke lay motionless until Jimmy's soft snores assured him he was asleep. As quietly as possible, he retrieved his stash from the dresser drawer—a roll of duct tape he had pilfered from the janitor's closet and a plastic bag. After one last affectionate gaze at Jimmy, he slipped out the door.

＝‖‖＝

Jimmy slept fitfully. He rose to go to the toilet. In the glimmer of the small night-light he saw Luke's chair and bed were empty.

"Dr. Brady." He lurched to the bathroom. Dark and unoccupied. "Dr. Brady." Walking as fast as he could without causing a disturbance, he went to the dining room. Deserted. The chapel. Empty. Maybe he's in the courtyard. He clomped down the hallway, steadying himself with the railing along the wall. He opened the door to the trash room.

"Dr. Brady—no—stop!"

Luke was struggling with a strip of duct tape, which was stuck to his fingers and to one side of the plastic bag pulled over his head. Other bits of tape clung to the side of his neck and his shirt. A half-empty roll lay at his feet.

Jimmy staggered to him and ripped the bag from his head. "You stupid asshole!" he yelled. "What are you thinking?"

He fumbled to peel off the bits of tape. Awkwardly, he gathered the tape and bag and dropped them in the trashcan. Luke made no move to resist when Jimmy jerked him from the stack of milk cartons, dragged him back to their room, and dumped him onto the bed. Drenched with sweat, Jimmy stood gasping.

"I've got to get Mrs. Graham," he said.

He almost fell when Luke grabbed the waistband of his pajamas and jerked him back. Jimmy panted until he regained his breath.

"Then I have to call Julie."

Luke's eyes were frantic. He grasped the front of Jimmy's pajama top, pulled him close, and violently shook his head. After a few moments, he loosened his hold and tried to smooth his shirt.

Jimmy threw his arms around Luke, and burying his face in Luke's chest, he began to sob softly. "Dr. Brady, what am I supposed to do? Pops died. My daddy didn't want me. You're the only father I've ever known. I can't lose you."

Luke gently patted his shoulder until he quieted. Jimmy blotted his eyes with his handkerchief and blew his nose.

"If I don't tell them, do you promise never to do this again?"

Luke looked directly into his eyes, drew an X across his chest with his finger, and nodded.

"You won't hurt yourself?"

Another X, and he shook his head.

Satisfied, Jimmy pressed Luke back onto the bed and pulled the covers up.

"OK, then, let's get some sleep." He paused a moment. "I'm sorry I called you an asshole."

━≺┼ ┼≻━

Rachel tiptoed in. Luke snored softly. Jimmy sat slumped in the chair at his side.

"Jimmy," she whispered.

His head jerked up.

"Everything all right?"

"Yes, ma'am, Dr. Brady's fine. He said to thank you for the cookies."

She put the dishes and remaining cookies on the tray. "I'd better get these back before Miss Benson comes in."

Jimmy went to his table, retrieved his cell phone, and took a folded sheet of paper from the drawer. As quietly as possible, he walked out. In the trash room, he unfolded the paper. He entered a number, then stepped out into the courtyard when it began to ring.

"Hello, Miss Brady, this is Jimmy at Shadydale."

⛝⛝

Jimmy rose and walked to the entrance for the fourth time. It was only two in the afternoon, but he had been sitting in the lobby since breakfast. When he made his predawn call, Mary said she would come as soon as possible. How long does it take to drive from Nashville?

"Thank goodness," he said aloud when he saw her striding up the walkway. He met her before she got to the door.

"Thank you for calling, Jimmy. How is he?"

"OK, I think. He promised not to do it again." Jimmy hesitated. "But I'm still scared."

"Me too," Mary said.

"He got real depressed after Julie got mad and quit visiting. Tonight I thought he was better. Then this." Jimmy's chin began to quiver. "I should have watched him better."

Mary laid her hand on his arm. "It's not your fault. You did all you could." He seemed mollified.

"Where is he?" Mary said.

"In our room."

Mary started toward the door, but Jimmy grabbed her by the arm.

"He's going to be mad I called you. Nobody knows but you and me."

She smiled at him. "Don't you worry. You did the right thing. I'll make everything all right."

Luke sat staring out the window, reviewing the evening's events. Jimmy was right. He was a stupid asshole. Who would have thought killing yourself could be so difficult? Especially for a doctor. But he had no gun. Couldn't get pills lethal enough to do the job. The silverware was too dull to cut his wrists. With only one fully functional hand, he couldn't possibly hang himself. A plastic bag and tape seemed his best option. If only he had gone to the far end of the dark courtyard, Jimmy would never have found him. But it was raining, so he stayed in the trash room. He snorted. He wanted to die, but he wanted to die warm and dry.

The tap on his door interrupted his musings. He gave Mary a quizzical look. "Win?" *What are you doing here?*

She walked to him and hugged him. "Jimmy called me early this morning."

His jaw clenched and his face clouded.

"Don't you dare say a word to that boy. He loves you dearly, and you frightened him to death." She let this sink in. "He did the right thing. He probably saved your life, however you might feel about it right now."

He gazed out the window, reluctant to make eye contact.

"How are you?"

A shrug.

"I talked with Julie this morning."

His head jerked back, a look of panic in his eyes.

"She told me about her visit with you."

He sighed and gazed skyward.

"I'm going to see her tonight. I'm going to tell her everything."

He spun around, waggled his head wildly, and struggled to rise. "Win!" *No! No! You can't.*

She slammed him back into his chair and shook him—hard—two, three, four times. "Lucas Brady, sit your butt down and listen to me."

His eyes widened. Mary using coarse language? Then he began to laugh, raised his hands in surrender, and sank back into his chair.

Stifling a giggle, she sat on the edge of the bed and grasped his hands in hers.

"Now that we know who's the boss..." her voice softened, "we really need to talk."

She took a deep breath. "Luke, this must end—the secrets, the deception, the lies. It destroyed Helen. It almost killed you; if you had succeeded, then it would have destroyed Julie, too. I refuse to be part of this charade any longer. I'm going to tell her everything."

He slumped back in the lounge chair, laid his arm across his eyes and nodded.

"Julie's a remarkable person. She's only heard a part of the truth, and that from Helen's viewpoint. When she learns the full story, I think she will understand, at least in part, why you and Helen did what you did."

He dropped his hands, gave her a forlorn look, and slowly shook his head.

"Don't sell her short. Deep down, she adores you. In time she will forgive you."

He continued to shake his head. His chest heaved with silent sobs. She cradled him in her arms and stroked his hair until he quieted.

She rose. "Pray for me, little brother; pray for all of us."

She kissed him on the forehead and left.

CHAPTER SIXTEEN

"You going to eat dinner?" Jimmy asked. "We're already late."
Luke had been staring out the window since Mary left. Jimmy
had popped in and out, obviously worried, but saying nothing. Had
he not been so upset, he would have found Jimmy's spastic attempt to
walk on eggshells comical. With a sigh, he nodded and rose, picked
up two medical journals, and followed him to the dining room.

Luke finally pushed his chair back, leaving most of his dinner
uneaten. He saw Jimmy staring at his piece of chocolate pie. He
smiled and slid it toward him. He held up the journals and pointed
toward the chapel, the only place of even minimal privacy. Jimmy
barely glanced up from the pie as he left.

He willed himself to read every page of the journals, even the
ads. Anything to keep his mind occupied. He flipped the last page,
laid them aside, slumped back on the pew and allowed his mind to
wander. Scenes from that terrible day, suppressed for twenty-five
years, swept over him.

⚔⚔

Seven-year-old Luke waved at him from the end of the dock and held up a stringer with four bluegills.

"All right, way to go," Luke shouted and started down the hill, only to be stopped short by his beeper. He sighed when he saw the phone number of the emergency room. "Be back in a sec," he called over his shoulder and trotted to the phone in the kitchen.

"Dr. Brady," the ER nurse said, "Tim Wilson has fallen, and it looks like he broke his arm."

Luke glanced at his watch. Helen should be back soon. "Go ahead and X-ray it. I'll be there in half an hour."

"Should we splint it?"

"That's fine."

"Wait, don't hang up," she went on. "Mitzi says three more are checking in. Hold on, and I'll see what's wrong."

"No need to, I'll be there in a few minutes," Luke snapped, but she had gone. He drummed his fingers on the countertop and shifted from one foot to the other. Finally, she returned.

"There's a forty-year-old lady with a headache, a twelve-year-old with a rash—"

"Are any of them serious?" Luke cut her off.

"Well, no. The third one has a wasp sting."

"I'll get there as soon as I can," he said, gritting his teeth. *God, some people are so anal.*

He started toward the lake. Young Luke wasn't on the dock.

"Hey, Lukie," he shouted. No answer. He trotted around the end of the house. "Lukie, come show me your fish." Nothing.

He ran to the dock. "Oh no," A knot tightened in his stomach when he spied the rod and reel in about six feet of water. "Lukie," he shouted even louder, his voice panicky. "God, please let him be OK."

He sprinted to the phone and dialed 911.

"Nine-one-one emergency, may I help you?"

"Katie, this is Dr. Brady. I think Luke has fallen in the lake. Get the rescue squad here STAT!"

He was wallowing in chest-deep water when the red truck roared up. Jack Jordan jumped from the truck. "You guys get the boat in the water."

Luke slogged up to him. "Jack, I was only inside for five or ten minutes; then he was gone."

"Slow down, Dr. Brady. When did you see him last?"

"About twenty minutes ago."

"Have you checked the grounds?"

"He's not there," Luke said.

Jack ran to the boat with Luke two steps behind. When Luke tried to clamber aboard, Jack shoved him back.

"Dr. Brady, please, let us do our job."

Luke nodded, stepped back, and watched as they began to drag the cove, grid by grid.

"Luke, what's wrong?" Helen fought her way through the growing crowd of onlookers.

He put his arms around her. "It's Lukie."

"What happened?" her voice rose.

"He was fishing off the dock. I had to answer the phone. When I came back, he was gone."

She jerked free and saw the boat in the cove. "Oh God, no!" she shrieked. She ran to the water's edge and slumped in a heap.

He followed her and tried to hold her.

"Get away from me. All you had to do was watch him for one hour."

The dragging went on and on. The crowd grew as news of the incident spread. The local TV station arrived.

Luke stared, transfixed by the boat methodically crossing and recrossing the cove. After about two hours, the crowd noise hushed at the sound of a shout from the rescue squad. All eyes riveted on the boat as they pulled the small limp figure from the water.

"No. No." Luke fell to his knees. His cry was drowned out by Helen's keening wails.

⟞⟨⊢ ⊣⟩⟝

Luke plodded about the yard in dazed silence, barely noticing Peter Hendricks, his pastor, trudging by his side. He jerked to a stop and looked wildly at the dock.

"His rod and reel. I've got to get Lukie's rod and reel."

Before Peter could say anything, Luke dashed to the dock and leaped into the water. He grabbed the rod and splashed to the shore. Not until he began reeling in the line did he notice the red and white bobber jiggling several yards out. When the line drew taut, he could feel the heavy yanking of a large fish. He cranked the reel with grim determination.

Finally a huge catfish, perhaps twenty pounds, floundered at the water's edge. With a heave Luke hurled it onto the shore. Wide mouth opening and closing, it fixed Luke with its dull eyes. Luke glared back. *You bastard. Either you pulled Lukie into the water or he got so excited he fell in.* Luke scrambled to the toolshed and grabbed an eight-pound sledge. He felt a pleasing crunch as the sledge smashed into the fish's head. "Ahhh!" he screamed and slammed the sledge down again and again until, exhausted, he slumped, gasping and sobbing. Bits of smelly flesh and entrails clung to his arms, face, and clothes. The bloody mush remaining was unrecognizable as a fish.

That night he had his first nightmare.

⟞⟨⊢ ⊣⟩⟝

Julie poured tea for Mary, Mark, and herself, then sat down.

"This is unexpected, Aunt Mary. Is something wrong?" she asked.

Mary sipped her tea, then took a deep breath. "Something's been wrong for a long time. I hope to set it right."

Julie set down her cup. "What do you mean?"

"First things first," Mary said. "Your father tried to kill himself last night."

"Oh no!" Julie gasped. "Is he all right?"

"Sad, depressed, embarrassed, but all right," Mary said. "He begged me not to tell you, but I told him I would have no part of any more secrets, lies, and deception."

"What do you mean?"

"It's a long story," Mary said. "Please hear me out. Then I'll try to answer any questions you may have."

Julie nodded assent.

"You must keep in mind: your parents are both good, wonderful people who had to deal with unbearable stress."

"What stress?" Julie asked.

"You had a brother," Mary began.

Julie's eyes widened.

"He drowned seven months before you were born. He was seven years old. His name was Luke. It almost destroyed them both."

Julie started to speak, but Mary held up her hand.

"Helen blamed your father. She destroyed every trace of little Luke she could find—pictures, toys, clothes—she burned them all. Whether she just couldn't tolerate any reminders, or she wanted to punish Luke, or both, I don't know."

Mary paused, her eyes far away. "She became severely depressed. She tried to drown herself in the same lake as little Luke. They had no choice except to commit her to a mental institution in Atlanta."

"She said she had to go there to be near her doctors because her pregnancy was so difficult."

"That's probably how she remembers it. Her pregnancy went fine; her mental state not so. She was psychotically depressed and suicidal. She had electroshock therapy three times. It played havoc with her memory."

"My God," Julie said.

"What about Daddy and that woman?"

"That's not excusable, but it's understandable. I think it was a result of his sorrow and loneliness. Helen refused to see him. He'd lost everything—little Luke, Helen. He was struggling to shut down his practice. Helen made it clear she would never return to Buxton."

Mary sighed and continued. "Karen was a receptionist at his office. She had lost a daughter three years before. She was the only person who had any idea what he was going through. I think he was simply desperate for any understanding. It just happened. A friend of Helen's told her about it. Karen moved back to West Virginia."

After a long pause, Julie spoke. "Why did they get back together?"

"You...and Luke's guilt." Mary's voice hardened. "He came crawling back and begged for forgiveness. Hell, he's spent the last twenty-five years trying to atone for his mistake. He only demanded one thing. He was going to raise you. Helen knew her psychiatric history would almost certainly prevent her from getting custody if they divorced. She agreed to come back, provided everything—little Luke, her illness, Luke's affair—be kept secret."

"Then she wanted me, too?" Julie asked.

"Yes, Julie. She wanted you. She loved you as best she could."

"As best she could?"

Mary bit her lip. "Luke's affair, your birth, and probably some genetic predisposition triggered a severe postpartum depression so severe she was readmitted and received two more shock treatments. I took a leave of absence and came to help with you. It took six months for her to stabilize. By that time, Luke had moved to Atlanta and started to work at the medical school."

The tea was cold. Mary stood, stretched, poured a cup, and reheated it in the microwave. Returning to her seat she continued.

"There's just a little more. Julie, you've taken a good bit of psychology. When is the most critical time in maternal-child bonding?"

Julie's eyes widened. "The first six months."

"Yes, the first six months. Luke and I were your sole caregivers and nurturers during that significant period. Helen physically and mentally could not help."

Julie nodded. "Is that why I've always felt closer to you and Daddy?"

"Probably, but Helen has done the best she could. She really tried to be a loving mother. She loved you enough that she went back to a man she found repugnant, unfaithful, and, in her mind, responsible for the death of her child. Maybe it was the electroshocks. Maybe she just can't allow herself to be vulnerable again. I don't know. Sometimes people build walls to fend off hurt and pain, but these same walls also repel love, compassion, and forgiveness."

They sat in silence for several minutes.

"You've dropped a load on me, Aunt Mary," Julie said. "I think I'm glad. I just don't know what to do with it."

"You have to decide how to deal with it," Mary said. "Just remember, they're good people. They both love you dearly. But Helen can't show it, and Luke can't say it."

CHAPTER SEVENTEEN

Luke slipped from his bed into his lounge chair, taking care not to wake Jimmy. Sleep was elusive, often impossible, since Mary had stated her intentions to tell all. This sure wouldn't improve his relations with Julie. Would Helen relapse, go crazy again, or just get angrier? How could he make Rachel understand his behavior back then and why he had cut her off with no explanation?

"You caused quite a stir last week."

Luke jumped when Gabe spoke from the open door. "How did you know about that? Did Jimmy tell you?"

"I have never met Jimmy."

"Then how did you know?"

Gabe sighed. "I'm here enough to know what's going on." After a long silence, he continued. "What did you think you'd accomplish?"

"I'm tired. My career's down the crapper. Julie hates me. No one would miss me anyway."

"Martin wouldn't miss you?" Gabe asked. "Mary wouldn't miss you? Jimmy wouldn't miss you? Julie wouldn't miss you?"

Luke squirmed. "Well…I…I—"

"You gave up. You quit." Gabe finished Luke's sentence. "You were sad," he said mockingly, "so you quit. I don't like quitters."

"OK, Mr. Know-It-All, what would you do in my place?" Luke snapped.

"I wouldn't quit. I'd work my tail off to do whatever good I could with whatever skills I had left."

"What skills?"

"You're a superb diagnostician and teacher. Dr. Brown said so."

"And where do I use these superb skills in this monotonous, smelly hellhole? Benson barred me from diagnosing and teaching or even reviewing patients' charts. Or hadn't you heard?"

"Go back to visiting. You listen. Everyone talks, but very few listen."

"I'm tired," Luke said.

Unperturbed, Gabe continued. "Most of all, I'd hang on to hope."

"Hope for what?"

Gabe laid his hand on Luke's arm. "You have to answer that, but hope is a good thing, a vital thing."

He stood.

"Don't go," Luke said, "it's been so long since I talked with someone."

"I'd like to stay, but I gotta get back to work," Gabe said.

"Come back and talk to me again. Please," Luke said.

"I'll stop by on my break when I can." Halfway to the door, he paused and turned to Luke. "You might want to try a little more of that prayer thing Mary mentioned," he said and left.

Luke looked at Jimmy, who hadn't moved. Couldn't he hear all of this conversation? Who was this Father Gabe? Luke had wrestled to understand this since his first visit. Since Gabe came only at night, was he some sort of realistic dream? His nightmares still left him in a cold sweat, yet he knew they weren't real. Maybe

Gabe wasn't, either. Maybe it was just his subconscious trying to sort out what was happening. The stroke had obviously scrambled his brain chemistry. Could this just be some sort of schizoid hallucination? He remembered a movie about a schizophrenic Nobel Prize–winning mathematician who learned to recognize his hallucinations and differentiate them from real people. Could he do that with Gabe? But, whatever Gabe might or might not be, he was right. Luke had to get off his butt and try to do something—he just didn't know what.

Two weeks later, he still didn't know. He stared out the window. As with most physicians, Luke's greatest fear was not being in control. He was haunted by the undiagnosed patient who got progressively worse, or the diagnosed patient who crashed despite the proper treatment. It was like that now. He couldn't speak and couldn't do anything to make the situation better. The revelation of more betrayals would drive Julie further away. Even if he could speak, what would he say? *I'm sorry.* Or just, *Please forgive me.* If she didn't, then what? He couldn't control Julie. He couldn't control the results of his stroke. What could he control?

In the past, when faced with tough decisions, he would write a list of every option he could think of. Then he would construct columns of the pros and cons of each option. When the exercise was completed, the best choice was usually obvious. But now he couldn't write. He tried doing the drill in his head, but the options, pros, and cons darted erratically through his brain, repeated themselves, bounced off one another, and intertwined in a mishmash of jumbled ideas. Finally, exhausted, he reached one conclusion. The only thing he could control was what he did.

He quit trashing his antidepressants. Maybe recent events and the changes the stroke caused in his brain chemistry wouldn't have plunged him so deeply into depression if he hadn't been so petulant and refused to take them. Besides, what were two more pills added to the five he was already taking?

His most urgent task was to make up with Rachel. Since his evening of temporary insanity, he had studiously avoided her. He made sure he was in bed with the lights out when she came on duty and waited until she had left in the morning before going to breakfast.

She and Jimmy were his only confidants in Shadydale. How could he have dumped her the way he did? How could he explain or apologize adequately with only facial expressions, hand motions, and pantomime to express himself? He needed to talk, but *win* wouldn't do the job. At the very least, he needed to write his reasons, but he could only scribble. What to do?

⚶

Luke surveyed the break room. He had cleaned the table except for two cups, two saucers, and a plate with four huge muffins he'd had Debbie purchase at a local bakery. He wore his nicest shirt and slacks. His lab coat was freshly cleaned and starched. He mentally practiced his carefully planned apology. The coffee maker gurgled as the last bit drained into the pot. Its aroma filled the room.

"Dr. Brady?"

He spun around. Rachel stood in the doorway, looking puzzled. He rushed to her and threw his arms around her, his prepared presentation a total blank. Realizing what he was doing, he stepped back. *I'm so sorry. I'm so sorry*, he mimed over and over. His hands fluttered as if each had a separate agenda.

She took his hand and led him to the table. "Sit down." She smiled. "I'll get the coffee. You're in no condition to pour." She sat and eyed the muffins. "Orange-cranberry—my favorite. Thank you."

I'm so sorry, he motioned again.

"Luke Brady, if you say 'I'm sorry' one more time, I'll throw your muffin in the trash and eat the other three in front of you."

Involuntarily, he laughed, spread his hands, and motioned, *OK, OK.*

They sipped and ate in silence.

"Jimmy told me about Julie. I'm so sorry. He said you'd been horribly depressed.

Luke nodded and silently sighed in relief. Jimmy hadn't told her about the plastic bag and tape.

"Are you any better?"

He paused in thought. Was he? *Yes,* he nodded. *Yes.*

"I'm so glad. I wanted to talk with you, but Jimmy thought that might hinder more than help." She paused. "He's very intuitive, very wise."

Luke nodded again.

Rachel told him about her mother and the latest scuttlebutt about Shadydale. Finally she rose. "Please come back. You don't know how much I've missed our morning visits." She took his hand and pressed it to her cheek. "Luke, you're very special to me. You don't have to fight all alone. I'm here."

His throat tightened. *Thank you,* he mimed.

<hr />

Luke resumed his visits with patients slowly at first. Two weeks later he was back on schedule. He had plenty of time. The patients and nurses welcomed him back. Whether because of the antidepressants or just his increased activity, he slept better. The nightmares came less often. His mood improved, nose-diving only when he dwelt on Julie. Mary kept reassuring him Julie would forgive him.

But would she? Could she? It would take time, Mary said. But how long? What about the baby? One uncertain question spawned a cascade of others. The only thing he knew to do was plunge back into work.

Finally convinced Luke was no longer a suicide risk, Jimmy spent more time with Debbie—Saturdays, Sundays, and whatever weekday time she could squeeze into her schedule.

For Luke, each day was a welcome challenge. His first visit today was with "Iron Mike" Hennessey, a decorated marine veteran of World War II and Korea, paraplegic since an auto accident a year ago.

"Come on in," he barked—an order, not a request. "How are ya, Doc?"

"Iron Mike" suited Gunnery Sergeant Hennessey perfectly: ramrod-straight in his wheelchair, lean, sinewy, GI haircut. Given a rifle, helmet, boots, and fatigues, he still looked capable of storming an enemy position even at eighty-eight years of age.

Luke smiled, then winced as Mike crushed his hand.

"Good to see ya. Sit down, Doc."

Luke sniffed and frowned. The putrid, fecal odor of pseudomonas hung like a pall over Mike.

"I know," he said. "It's enough to gag a maggot."

Luke gave him a questioning look.

"Hell, I was in Korea for eighteen months and got nothing more than a frostbit toe at the Chosin Reservoir. I'm here less than a year and have a rotting sore on my butt."

Luke motioned him up. Mike raised himself half up out of his seat. Luke lowered his pajamas, revealing a four-inch, runny, red ulcer over his tailbone.

Luke signaled him to sit and left. Spying Amy two doors down, he beckoned her to come.

"Mike, why didn't you say something?" she asked.

"Didn't want to bother you, ma'am."

Amy led Luke to an unoccupied room. "Dr. Brady, don't let Miss Benson catch you examining patients," she said.

Luke gave a dismissive wave.

"We'll get right on that," she said. "That's the fourth one this month. We have an excellent wound care team, but they can't keep up with these worn-out mattresses and stiff covers." She turned to go. "Remember what I said about Miss Benson."

⊷⊶

The next morning, Martin and Jimmy were finishing breakfast when Luke sat down and tossed a six-inch piece of brittle, rubberized material onto the table and stared at Martin.

"That broke off his mattress last night," Jimmy said.

"Luke, I'm doing everything I can."

Luke continued to stare.

"I tell them every month to do something. They just won't listen."

Luke snorted. Reaching across the table, he pulled off Martin's plastic picture ID badge.

Martin Brown, MD
Medical Director

Luke crumbled the mattress cover fragment, then tapped his finger, first on "Medical Director" then on Martin's chest.

Almost pleading, Martin said, "I told you before, if I do anything more, they'll fire me."

Luke continued to stare. He lifted a felt-tipped pen from Martin's coat. Deliberately, he crossed out MD on the name tag, laid the pen down, and walked away.

He found three more bedsores and left the charts for Jimmy to show Martin.

Martin, for his part, avoided Luke. He started rounds when he arrived and skipped their morning meetings over breakfast and coffee.

⚓

A week later, Luke and Jimmy were putting finishing touches to breakfast.

"You want your toast and jelly?" Jimmy asked as he removed them from Luke's plate.

Luke smiled and shook his head. A grim-faced Martha glared at them as she strode by—no greeting, no snide remarks, no wink.

"Looks like the queen has a bee in her bonnet," Jimmy whispered.

Luke laughed and gave him an exaggerated wink.

Jimmy swallowed the last bit of toast. "I wonder if Dr. Martin is sick," he said. "He wasn't here Thursday or Friday. I don't remember the last time he missed one day, much less two."

As if in answer to his question, ten minutes later Martin strolled in, coffee in hand.

"Morning, Luke, Jimmy," he said with an ebullient smile.

"Are you OK?" Jimmy asked.

"I'm fine. Better than fine," Martin said.

"Why?" Jimmy persisted.

"I took a trip to Atlanta."

"What did you do?" Jimmy asked.

"Something I should have done a long time ago." He looked at Luke. "You were right. I'm a doctor. A doctor looks after his patients' needs before his own." He sipped his coffee. "I visited Shadydale's corporate headquarters. They had no idea of the situation here. Crandell and Benson have received funding for almost two hundred mattresses and covers over the last year. None have been purchased. We will receive seventy-five this week, seventy-five next month, and the rest the month after that."

Luke beamed and slapped him on the back.

Martin went to the urn and refilled his cup. "That's not all," he said. "I explained our previous setup and the way it improved patient care. I'm no longer on probation." He paused. "Benson's on probation now."

Luke gave a low whistle.

"Yeah," Martin said more seriously. "I'd watch out for her. She'll blame this as much on you as on me." He smiled again. "There's more." He beamed at their expectant gazes. "As of tomorrow morning, Luke, you are reinstated as the unpaid clinical assistant to the medical director with all perks and privileges thereof—if you want the job."

Stunned, Luke sat motionless.

"Well?" Martin said.

Luke nodded vigorously, synchronous with pumping Martin's hand.

"Tomorrow morning OK?"

Luke swallowed hard and mimed fervent thanks.

"No, Luke, thank you."

⋙⊢⊣⋘

He stood at the nurses' station looking like a proper physician—starched shirt and slacks and a fresh lab coat. A stethoscope hung around his neck. The charts of the fourteen patients he had seen were stacked neatly.

Martin beamed as he strode up. "Welcome back, Dr. Brady... uh, Luke," he corrected himself. Luke smiled, handed him the first chart and led him to a nearby room. Rounds went quickly.

Martin scribbled his signature to the last chart. "Wow! Lots of time. Let's get some coffee."

They sat in the empty day room, sipping coffee and scarfing huge cinnamon rolls. Martin tapped his pastry. "I'm glad you're back. They never gave me cinnamon rolls." He finished the last two bites, then left.

"Dr. Brady, you seem happy again," Jimmy said.

Luke smiled. The thought of seeing patients again invigorated him. When Lukie died and Helen pushed him away, the two things that gave his life meaning were practicing medicine and raising Julie. When Julie left for college, medicine was his anchor. With her gone again, medicine could rescue him once more.

≒┼┾

Luke plunged back into rounding and visitation. He desperately needed to stay busy. Morning rounds gave way to before-lunch visits. In the afternoon, he screened the next day's recerts, saw any problems the nurses found, and visited residents until dinner.

He and Lily had a standing book discussion date each Thursday after he wheeled her back from her singing engagement in the dementia unit. She had almost reached Jimmy's level of proficiency in interpreting his mimes and signs. He kept a notepad where he jotted the pages and paragraphs of parts he particularly liked or disliked. Sometimes he highlighted sections just because he knew Lily would disagree with them.

Lily's political and social views tended to be somewhat to the left of Karl Marx. Luke, on the other hand, was more middle-of-the-road, which was liberal by most doctors' standards. Lily considered him a reactionary conservative and often referred to him as a Luddite or a troglodyte. She clipped provocative articles and several letters to the editor she had written from her *New York Times* for him. Luke relished their arguments. He wondered if he could parry her rhetorical thrusts even if he had full command of his speech.

Luke succeeded in having almost no idle time during weekdays. With Jimmy gone most of the weekend, he couldn't manufacture enough activity to occupy all his spare time. During these empty intervals, and as he lay in bed at night, his thoughts turned to Julie.

CHAPTER EIGHTEEN

Luke sat in the warm April sun idly tossing bits of bread to five chittering sparrows.

"Daddy"

At the sound of Julie's voice, he spun around and stood, uncertain what to do.

She strode to him, leaning awkwardly to avoid her protruding belly, and threw her arms around him.

His eyes were moist as he patted her shoulder and stammered, "Win, win." *Julie, thank God, you're back.*

She stepped back, brushed a tear from her cheek, and put her finger to his lips.

"It's OK, Daddy. It's OK."

She sat on the bench and tugged him down beside her. "Aunt Mary told me everything."

His head drooped.

She grasped his hand. "Look at me." Her gaze was steady. "I can't say I'm happy with what you and Mother did. I'm still trying to make sense of it. I can't imagine what both of you went through.

I don't know what Mark and I would do if something like that happened to us. I just wish you could talk to me and help me understand. I've had two visits with Mother. For the first time ever, we talked—really talked. I think she's relieved this has come out into the open. She seems less bitter. She even made an appointment with a therapist. Maybe things will get better."

She hugged him again and gave him a brilliant smile. "I'm just glad we're back together again. All of us, including this little guy. He's due next week." She stood and placed Luke's hand on her abdomen. "Did you feel that? I think he may be a professional tap dancer."

She stretched, walked around, and again sat at Luke's side. "Mary told me about Mother destroying any trace she could find of little Luke." A wistful look came to her eyes. "I'd really like to know what my brother looked like."

Luke bit his lip and fumbled to retrieve his wallet. He unzipped the security pocket and with great care removed two faded photographs wrapped in tissue. He handed her the first, a typical black-and-white school picture of a smiling boy with dark hair, verging on curly. She inspected the picture. When she looked up, Luke held up six fingers.

"He was six?"

Luke nodded.

"This must be his first grade picture."

Another nod.

"He looks like you, except he has Mother's eyes."

She took the other photo, wallet-size and in color. Little Luke stood barefoot in cutoff jeans, smiling broadly, holding up a three-pound bass. He had sparkling blue eyes and curly brown hair.

Luke held up seven fingers.

Julie studied the pictures. "I hope my Luke is as good-looking."

Luke's heart skipped a beat. With all that had happened, he feared she had changed her mind on the baby's name.

She continued to pore over the pictures as they talked. The sun was setting when she rose.

"I have to go. I'm meeting Mother for dinner; have to keep the fence-mending momentum going." She held up the photographs. "Could I keep these for a while? They can do wonderful things restoring old pictures. These will be totally faded soon."

Luke stopped. He had a worried frown.

"I'll be careful with them."

Luke shook his head and waved his hand.

"What? Oh, I get it. I won't let Mother know about them just yet, although I don't think she would do anything."

She bent and kissed him on the cheek. "Daddy, we're going to be happy again. All of us, I promise." One last smile and she left.

CHAPTER NINETEEN

J immy picked up the jangling phone. "Hello." He listened a moment. "That's great. Here's Dr. Brady," he said and handed Luke
the receiver.

"Luke, this is Mark. I'm in the delivery room. Lucas Marcus
Vaccaro arrived at seven thirty-two. Seven pounds, nine ounces,
and twenty-three inches long. Looks like he's got the Brady height.
He and Julie are fine. Congratulations, Grandad."

"Win! Win! Win!" *That's wonderful. I'm so happy for all three of you.*

"Julie wants to talk with you."

"Daddy, he's beautiful. He looks just like Lukie."

Luke beamed.

"Aunt Mary is coming tomorrow. She'll pick you up tomorrow
morning. I can't wait for you to meet him."

⊶⊹⊹⊷

Luke laid the paper down and paced around the room again. He
had read the entire *Atlanta Journal-Constitution* and was on the

editorial page of Jimmy's *Wall Street Journal*. He didn't recall anything he had read. Where was Mary? She should be here.

"Dr. Brady," Jimmy said, "it's just nine fifteen. Mary said she'd be here around ten. Why don't you try to take a nap? You've been up since four."

Luke leaned back in his recliner and tried to relax. Sleep was impossible. He almost fell, scrambling up at Mary's knock.

She hugged him and stepped back. "You ready to go...?" Her voice trailed off as Luke disappeared through the door. She smiled and shrugged at Jimmy. "See you later."

⟞⟝

Mark's smile lit up the room as he shook Luke's hand, then hugged Mary. "I'm so glad you're here."

He led them to the bed where Julie cradled a wrinkled baby with long dark hair and dark-blue eyes.

Luke gasped. Julie had been right. He was Lukie reincarnate.

She handed him to Luke. "Say hello to your grandson, Daddy."

They had visited, oohed, and aahed for over an hour when the nurse entered.

"Miss Brady, Dr. Brady, it's feeding time. Then Julie must rest. You need to start wrapping things up."

"Daddy, I've got two things we need to go over before you leave," Julie said.

She walked to the closet and returned with a large picture.

"Aunt Mary had squirreled away some pictures of Lukie without Mother's knowledge. I made four of these." She handed him a collage of fourteen pictures, including the restored two Luke had given her. "I'm going to have several enlarged into eight-by-tens. I'll get you copies when they're ready."

Luke's throat tightened. His vision blurred. He nodded his thanks.

"I've already given one to Mother. She seemed so happy to get it. She was here last night and is coming back later today. I didn't know how she would react, but she seems thrilled with Lucas."

She handed the collage to Mary and took Lucas from Luke.

They chatted until Julie spotted the nurse standing impatiently in the doorway.

"I think you have to go," she said. "As soon as I get things settled, I want to bring Lucas to Shadydale. I'm sure Jimmy wants to see him."

Luke clapped Mark on the back and kissed Julie. Halfway to the door, he turned back, kissed Lucas once more, and hurried out.

CHAPTER TWENTY

J immy couldn't sit still or stop talking. "It's really nice of Julie to
bring little Lucas to see us. Do you think she'll let me hold him?
I've never held a baby before. What if I drop him?"

Luke smiled and motioned for him to calm down.

Jimmy laughed nervously. "I can't help it. I—"A knock on the
door interrupted him. "I'll get it."

Luke rose and did a doubletake as Julie, Lucas nestled in her
arms, walked in, followed by Helen. *What's she doing here?* Except
for times when she had business with Benson or Crandell, she had
only visited him twice in the seven months he'd been here. On
both occasions, after some superficial, strained small talk and awk-
ward silences, both visits ended quickly.

"Mother wouldn't hear of me driving down alone with Lucas,"
Julie said.

Luke and Jimmy rushed to get chairs for them.

"You look good, Luke," Helen said with a smile. "How are you
doing?"

Richard Dew

Her friendly smile and relaxed manner almost made him think she meant it. Uncertainly, he nodded.

"Sit down, Daddy," Julie said and placed Lucas in his arms. "Be prepared for accidents. He sucked me dry on the way here."

She took Jimmy's hand. "Jimmy, I'd like you to meet my mother, Helen," Julie said.

Jimmy shook her hand. "Pleased to meet you, Mrs. Brady."

"Julie tells me you have really looked after Luke. Thank you," Helen said.

The conversation centered mainly on Lucas.

Luke motioned to Julie.

"What is it, Daddy?"

He nodded to Jimmy.

Jimmy blushed. "He says can I hold the baby?"

"Of course," Julie said, transferring him from Luke to Jimmy.

"He's so small," Jimmy said. "I've never seen a baby up close before."

Luke was as taken by Helen as Jimmy was by Lucas. The icy reserve had melted. She spoke and laughed easily. Her whole countenance seemed different. The hard lines around her eyes and mouth were softer. She reminded Luke of the Helen he knew long ago.

"Jimmy," Helen said, watching Lucas suck on his finger, "Lucas seems to have really connected to you. You'd make a good nanny."

"He's really neat," Jimmy said. "Oh, I almost forgot. I told Maybelle about you coming. She said she'd bake us some muffins if she could see Lucas."

"What are we waiting for?" Helen said. "I missed breakfast. I'm starved." She took Lucas from Jimmy. "I'll carry Lucas, if you'll tote the muffins."

After they left, Julie sat beside Luke. "Mother has been very mysterious the last few days. I'm not sure what it's about, but she's been talking to people at the medical school."

What? Luke mimed.

"Maybe nothing. I guess we'll just have to wait and see if it's anything."

Helen and Jimmy's return ended further conjecture.

Whatever tension may have remained evaporated with the arrival of muffins and coffee. Julie and Helen joked easily with each other. Luke joined in warily.

⟩⟨

After they left, Luke pondered what, if anything, had happened. Was it just euphoria over the new baby? It seemed as if a corner had been turned, a milestone passed. But to what end? Would it last? Where might it lead?

⟩⟨

A week later Julie called.

"Daddy, remember when I said Mother was talking to people at the medical school? Well, she's set up a meeting for May 17. I'm still in the dark. I'll be down before lunch. I want you to look nice. That means coat and tie."

⟩⟨

May 17.

Luke inspected himself in the mirror. Despite himself, he burst out laughing and pointed at Jimmy. His tie hung in a tangled wad.

Jimmy began to giggle. "Well, it's better than the herky-jerky knot you did with your bum hand," he said.

This increased Luke's laughter, which, like a contagion, spurred Jimmy from giggles to guffaws.

When Julie walked in, they were slumped in their chairs, nearly breathless, with tears running down their cheeks.

"What in the world?" she asked.

Luke flipped the tangle of tie, which precipitated more gales of laughter.

Julie began to laugh also. "You two!" She grasped Luke's hand. "Stand up before your shirt and trousers look like your tie."

She removed the tie and retrieved a clip-on tie and a bow tie.

"Mark reminded me you hadn't worn a tie since the day of your stroke. These are Walmart specials, but they'll have to do for now." She held them up. "Which one?"

Luke pointed to the bow tie.

"I hoped you'd pick that one. It'll separate you from the herd."

Luke hunched forward, fingers held to the sides of his head like horns, pawed the floor with his foot, and again began laughing.

Julie couldn't suppress a smile. "You're right. You're a herd unto yourself, but at least this tie will give you class."

As he struggled into his blue blazer, Helen and Martin walked in.

"You look good, Luke," Helen said with a smile and kissed him on the cheek.

Surprised, he stiffened and shifted uneasily.

"Neat tie," Martin said. He looked at his watch. "We'd better get moving. They're waiting for us."

The three men rose when Martin ushered Luke, Helen, and Julie into the conference room. The shortest of the three motioned for everyone to sit.

"Mrs. Brady, Mrs. Vacarro, I'm Joe Wilkenson. I became dean by default when Dr. Brady became ill. This is Dr. Rosman, director of medical education, and this is Dr. Walden, chief financial officer." He smiled at Luke. "We three go a long way back with Dr. Brady. But we're here today as educators, not friends."

He motioned to Martin. "Luke, when Dr. Martin told us of your work with him here, we were intrigued. Despite our best efforts, our doctors in training seem to be drifting more and more toward depersonalized, technologically oriented medical practices. You were speaking of this very thing when you had your stroke." He paused and took a sip of water. "We are desperate to reemphasize the importance of the basics of good medicine: a thorough history and physical examination, of course, but also caring, compassionate, and personal relationships with our patients. Your work with the students we sent here earlier proved that not only could you still teach, but also that you could teach at an exceptional level. These students were blown away by the amount of information they were able to glean by paying attention to the physical exam. It's already showing up in their work. We'd like to make this a part of our curriculum."

He nodded to the tall, balding doctor beside him.

Dr. Rosman stood. "Dr. Brady, we have a proposal. We'd like you to rejoin our teaching staff. We feel this would be a great learning experience as well as an inspiration for our students. You would round with the students and residents five days a week in both the hospital and the university rehab center." He smiled toward Julie. "That would leave your weekends free to spend with your new grandson." He gave this a moment to sink in. "Luke, do you think you would be interested?"

Luke's hands trembled as he pumped his head in a vigorous assent.

"Good. Dr. Walden will give you the basics about the finances."

Dr. Walden remained seated and opened a folder. "We have arranged for a residential four-room suite in the rehab center or, if you prefer, we will provide an allowance for private housing. Your beginning salary will be nine thousand dollars a month plus full benefits. The initial contract is for one year. If all parties are satisfied, we will then renegotiate restoration of your tenure." He nodded toward Helen. "Mrs. Brady helped us develop this offer. I would have her negotiate any future deals if I were you. She drives a hard bargain."

He closed the folder.

The dean smiled toward Luke. "Still interested?"

Luke gave him an enthusiastic thumbs-up.

"Good. We only have a little over five months to get this done."

━━◁┼┼▷━━

Afterward in his room, Luke struggled to calm himself and to comprehend what had just happened. Wow! Springing this place and landing back at the medical center in one fell swoop. Working with the students, attending daily conferences, and socializing with the teaching staff was a dream come true. He might even get into that experimental speech therapy project.

A knock at the door broke his train of thought.

"May I come in?" Helen asked.

Had something gone wrong? He rose and motioned to her.

"No, no. Everything's OK," she said, recognizing his worried expression. "We...I just need to talk."

Luke motioned to his chair and sat on the edge of the bed. Helen seemed different. The changes he had noticed earlier remained. Her posture was less rigid. Her expression was softer. The edge was gone from her voice.

She pulled a handkerchief from her purse and, eyes downcast, toyed with it. She looked up and smiled. "I'm not good at this," she said with a nervous laugh. "I've been busy since Mary told Julie about..." She bit her lip. "Us."

After a long pause, she continued. "I'm going to a support group for bereaved parents, and I'm seeing a counselor. I've been angry and screwed up for a long time—ever since, you know, little Luke." She rolled her eyes. "God, it's still so hard to say his name."

He laid his hand on hers.

182

"My counselor says it might be time to make amends." She took a deep breath. "I think she's right."

Another long pause. Her gaze fixed somewhere out the window. She continued, seeming to speak as much to herself as to him. "I was so angry about everything: you, little Luke, my mental breakdowns, being pregnant, still being alive. Having you to blame gave me a focus for my anger. Then after *her*, a focus for my hate."

He hung his head. "Win." *I am so sorry.*

"I would have left you, but because of my mental state, I was afraid I would lose Julie. Then I lost her anyway." A tear ran down her cheek. "God, help me. I think I stayed just to punish you. But over so long a time, anger and hate get harder and harder to maintain. I am so tired. It must end."

He looked at her and spread his hands. "Win." *You don't have to do this.*

"No, let me finish. I've worked hard on this." She smiled. "You know, we had twelve wonderful years—even when we had only pork and beans and wieners to eat."

He gave an involuntary laugh.

She lifted the collage of Lukie from the table. "Julie gave me one, too. I love it. How could I have destroyed everything? I must have…" She laughed. "Gone crazy," she said with a wry smile. "And we had Luke for seven of those years. Now I'm trying to focus on his life, not his death."

You're right. Why haven't I ever thought of it that way?

She took his hands in hers and looked directly into his eyes. "Luke, I want to live, really live, the rest of my life. I want the same for you. I don't think I can forget, but I forgive you for whatever you may have done in an impossible situation. I hope you can forgive me."

He swallowed hard and slowly nodded. He took the damp handkerchief from her and dabbed first his eyes, then hers. They sat silently for several minutes.

Finally, she spoke. "There's two more things."

He sat back, a questioning look on his face.

"With the offer from the medical school, you have a future. I'd like one, too, but I can't find it here. There are too many ghosts, too many reminders. I need to get away. Probably permanently. My cousin in Dallas has asked me to come live with her. I need a new start. I know I need to remain in therapy. I have a job at a daycare center. If I enjoy it, I may go on and get into teaching."

Luke smiled and nodded his approval.

Helen picked up her purse and retrieved a folded document from it. She handed the papers to Luke. "This is yours."

He recognized his wobbly signature on the financial power of attorney.

"My lawyer says it's foolish to give this to you." She laughed softly. "Actually, he said it was insane. But I don't want it. I don't need it anymore. I never did."

Luke smiled gently.

Helen stood and walked to the window.

"Now comes the hardest part."

Luke's brow furrowed.

"I've filed for a divorce."

His head jerked around.

"Luke, I don't want to hurt you anymore. This is not about that. We haven't been husband and wife for twenty-five years. We may forgive each other, but we can't forget—too much has happened. We can't put it back together. We all know that. Even Julie. She doesn't like it, but she understands."

Luke bit his lip and then slowly nodded.

"Oh, I wish you could talk. I want to hear you say it's OK. I want you to understand."

She sat and took his hands in hers. "Our lives will always be 'before Lukie and after Lukie.' Let's try to remember the good 'before' times and put the bad 'after' times behind us. I'm convinced there are some good times left—for both of us."

After a long pause, she rose.

She bent, looked deeply into his eyes, and placed her hands on his cheeks.

"You're a good man, Luke. I knew that when I met you. I think I've always known it. Even though I wouldn't admit it when I thought I hated you."

Tears ran down her cheeks as she gently kissed him.

"Goodbye, Luke."

She left without looking back.

CHAPTER TWENTY-ONE

Jimmy closed his Bible and began pacing for the third time. Finally, he dragged his wooden desk chair to Luke and sat down. He seemed on the verge of tears. Luke laid his book aside. "Dr. Brady, I've got to talk with you. The words came out strained and jerky.

Luke nodded.

"Debbie and I want to get married."

Luke smiled and gave him thumbs-up.

"No, you don't understand. I'm not sure we should," Jimmy said.

Why? Luke mimed.

"We want to have children."

So?

Jimmy stared at the floor. His right foot tapped uncontrollably. His face was contorted more than usual.

"Would they be like me? You know..." He passed his hand from head to toe. "Like this?"

Luke shook his head and waved his hand from side to side. *No! No! No!*

"Are you sure? Miss Benson said they would."

Luke's face turned red. His fists pounded the arms of his chair. He shook his head no four, five, six times. How could she say that? How could she be so cruel? She knew better. Was she trying to get at him through Jimmy?

"You promise?" Jimmy asked.

Luke smiled, nodded, and crossed his heart.

Jimmy threw his arms around him. "Thank you, Dr. Brady, thank you."

What does Debbie think? Luke mimed.

Jimmy laughed. "She says the queen bee is full of beans."

Luke burst out laughing and nodded his head in agreement.

"So you think it's a good idea?" Jimmy asked.

Another nod. Luke patted his hip pocket and mimed taking his wallet out.

"Money?" Jimmy said. "No problem."

He retrieved his laptop. "I'll show you something if you promise not to tell anybody."

Luke gave him an incredulous look.

Jimmy poked him on the arm. "You know what I mean."

He opened a spreadsheet. "I took some online courses on investing. This is why I read the *Wall Street Journal* every day. He pointed to a sum dated fourteen years previously: $776,431. "That's what my mother left me. The interest paid for me to stay at Shadydale. The amount actually increased a little each year. Here's where I started investing," he said, indicating a point nine years ago. "I beat the market seven out of nine years." He smiled. "Here's where I was last month: $2,017,322."

Luke whistled.

"Like I said, money's no problem." He paused a moment. "Debbie will finish her nursing training in ten months. She won't need to work, but she's always dreamed of being a nurse. She'd love to work here, but queen bee may not let her."

Luke pointed to Jimmy with a questioning look.

"Me? For now, I want to keep visiting my friends and helping Dr. Brown. We're looking for a house close enough for me to walk." He gave a rueful laugh. "I wouldn't want to ride in a car with me for a driver."

━⟨┼⟩━

Except for eating meals, visiting, and making rounds with Martin, Luke sought what solitude he could find and pondered what had happened and what it meant. The divorce was final four days ago. He felt a deep relief, yet a simultaneous overwhelming sense of sadness. He was on an emotional trampoline. Anticipation of his return to the medical school verged on euphoria. A reporter from the *Atlanta Journal-Constitution* interviewed Dr. Wilkerson about Luke's return. He would be "an inspiration to all stroke victims and a stirring example for the medical students," the article read.

From these highs, he would, for no obvious reason, plummet into a morass of could haves and should haves he had for so long successfully suppressed. Like a tennis ball dropped onto the pavement, he rebounded from each emotional plunge. But like the ball, each rebound was less high, and each descent came with increasing frequency. Despite the antidepressants, his emotions ground inexorably downward. Sleep eluded him. When he did sleep, the nightmares returned. Thoughts of the trash room and plastic bags popped up at odd times.

━⟨┼⟩━

Luke skipped visiting this afternoon and slipped into the deserted chapel. He ought to be happy, but he was an emotional train wreck. He began again trying to sort out Helen, Rachel, Lukie, the return to the medical school, his affair, his future, but his thoughts fragmented into a disjointed, jumbled mess. Finally, in desperation, he tried to pray.

"Win." *God...I...I...Dammit, I need help. Where the hell are You?*

"Hey, that's good, Luke—honest, from the heart."

Luke spun around. "Father Gabe, how long have you been there?"

"I just slipped in," Gabe said. "What's the problem?"

"I don't know," Luke said. "I'm getting out of this place. I'm getting my job back, things are settled with Helen, I should be on top of the world, but I'm not. It just hurts too much to stop hurting."

"Why do you think that is?" Gabe asked.

Luke clenched and unclenched his fists. "I just can't let it go."

"Let what go?"

"I let Lukie die. I betrayed Helen. I violated everything I said I stood for: my family, my faith."

"Listen to yourself, Luke. Lukie's death was an accident—a tragedy—but an accident. You fouled up big-time with Helen, but you repented. You spent half your life seeking atonement. She's sincerely forgiven you. And, God, He forgave you years ago." He paused, letting this sink in. "When are you going to let yourself off the hook?"

"But..."

"But nothing," Gabe snapped. "Suppose you and Jimmy traded places, and he had done precisely what you did. Suppose he confessed this to you. Would you tell him, 'You're right, Jimmy, you're a faithless, philandering killer who deserves to be miserable'?"

"Of course not," Luke said.

"So this forgiveness bit is good enough for everyone else, even God, but not good enough for you? Isn't it the height of egotistical hubris to hold yourself to an unattainable moral standard and the rest of humankind to a more possible one?"

"I never thought of it in that way," Luke said.

"Well, think about it."

They sat in silence for several minutes.

"You're right," Luke said. "I'll work on it."

Gabe nodded and smiled. "It looks like things are turning around for you."

"How did you know?"

Gabe rolled his eyes.

Before he could reply, Luke laughed and blurted, "Yes, yes, you make it your business to keep up with what's going on here. I keep forgetting."

"Will you be happy?"

Again Luke paused. "I think so. I can't wait to get back in the medical school. I think I can teach the students something. It will be good to be back with my friends."

"What about your friends here?"

"Friends might be the wrong word. I don't think I've ever had but one close friend. I've had many colleagues, but no one I could relate to heart-to-heart. Someone who really understood me. Other than Helen for a while, I've never known anyone else like that." He paused; his eyes widened. "Except Jimmy…and Rachel."

Gabe nodded.

"But I can come back and visit them. Rachel and I can commute back and forth."

"Hmm," Gabe murmured uncertainly. "Maybe you have to be a friend to have a friend."

"You're right, but I'm sure I can do more good there than here. Besides, I can get back into the experimental speech therapy program."

"Yes, you can. Do you think it might help?"

Luke sighed. "Probably not."

They sat in silence.

"Do you ever go to the university hospital?" Luke asked.

"I go where I'm told."

"I'd really like to see you again."

"You never know," Gabe said. He rose to leave. "You've got a lot of thinking to do, Luke."

"I know. It can be overwhelming."

Gabe smiled. "You might want to talk it over with my boss."

"What do you mean?"

"You know, like you were when I came in," Gabe said, pointing his finger upward.

Luke nodded. "You're right. I've already started."

"Good luck," Gabe said and left.

Luke returned to the chapel daily. His only prayer was, *God, help me get this right*. His moods stabilized. The highs were more realistic. The lows moderated. Thoughts of Lukie still blindsided him, but, afterward, he didn't drop as deep or remain down for as long as previously. Maybe, bit by bit, he was letting himself off the hook.

With his improved mental outlook, Luke began preparing for the move to the medical center. He reviewed his texts and sorted the papers he and Martin had accumulated teaching students. The hump he couldn't get over was how could he communicate with the students? They wouldn't understand what Jimmy called their "ape-man talk." He couldn't take Jimmy with him. With only three months left, could he do it?

CHAPTER TWENTY-TWO

L uke had always been a private person, a loner. Throughout his medical career, he had the innate ability to inspire trust in his patients. They freely shared their anxieties, apprehensions, and failures. But with Luke, as with many men, sharing was a one-way street. He was more likely to bare his body than one small bit of his soul. He had no true confidants among his colleagues. Like most of them, he buried his secret inner life deep, leaving only medicine, sports, politics, gossip, and weather as topics for conversation.

Helen was the only person with whom he had ever been open and honest about his inner life—his hopes, his dreams, his fears, his weaknesses. In some way he couldn't explain, she seemed interested, caring, and safe.

After their estrangement, he had no significant female relationships. His association with women was superficial. He knew, liked, and was liked by, most of the female nursing staff at the medical school. He was closest to Lauren Levin in the ICU, but they shared few confidences, and most of their discussions consisted of lighthearted banter and brief, inconsequential conversations about family.

That changed when Rachel came to Shadydale. She made him laugh, and more importantly, made him feel at ease. She didn't seem put off by his inability to talk and had been quick to pick up on the pantomimes, facial expressions, and body language he and Jimmy had concocted. He enjoyed their early-morning visits, even more now that she worked Saturday and Sunday, leaving time for leisurely breakfasts together. Since the divorce, she was more willing to be seen in public with him. They had platonic dinner dates. She called him Luke except when around others at work.

This morning she joined him for breakfast.

"How many neurosurgeons does it take to screw in a lightbulb?" she asked.

Luke shrugged and shook his head.

"Just one," she said and paused, ignoring his expectant look. "He holds the bulb and the world revolves around him."

Luke clapped his hands and burst out laughing.

After he quieted, she spoke hesitantly. "Dr. Brady, I know sign language. Maybe that's why I understand you as well as I do. I could teach you."

His face tightened. He shook his head and waved his hand.

"Please, try for me."

He sighed and nodded.

"Now, you do just as I do. This is an L." She waited. "Come on, try it."

He signed the L.

"This is a U."

He signed the U, and the K, and the E she showed next.

"L-U-K-E," she signed slowly. "Now you try it."

He looked helplessly at his unmoving hands, then rose and walked away.

"Luke, wait. I'm sorry."

He held up his hand, smiled reassuringly, and walked to the table where Jimmy and Debbie sat. He motioned, and Jimmy followed him back to Rachel.

"I was trying to teach him sign language," Rachel said.

"Forget it," Jimmy said. "They tried that a long time ago. Didn't work. They said it was like Dr. Brady's writing. He recognizes the letters. He can even copy them, but his stroke won't let him make them into words on his own."

"Drat!" Rachel said after Jimmy left. "I'm determined for you to tell me how smart and pretty I am."

Luke laughed, then pointed at her, framed his smiling face, and pointed to his head. He repeated the series.

"OK, OK, I get it," she said. "You said, 'You're pretty and smart.' Thank you, but that's not exactly what I wanted."

⚔

Two days later, Luke was so engrossed in his newspaper that he didn't hear Rachel enter the break room.

She paused and watched. Whenever he wasn't busy, he seemed to be reading: the paper, his Bible, medical journals. An idea that had been sloshing around in her mind began to gel.

"You don't have any trouble reading, do you?" she asked.

Luke shook his head and smiled.

She poured herself a cup of coffee and set it on the table.

"What are you reading?" she asked.

He held up the newspaper.

"No, which newspaper is it?"

He looked puzzled, then turned to the front page and pointed to the large header: *Atlanta Journal-Constitution*.

"What's the date?"

He frowned.

"No, seriously, what's the date?"

He rolled his eyes and pointed to the date at the top of the page: Friday, May 29, 2015.

"What's your favorite baseball team?"

Another eye roll, then he turned to the sports section and pointed: "Braves win 4–2." He gave her a questioning look and shrugged his shoulders.

"Probably nothing," she said. "I'll tell you about it later. I'm going to be busy tomorrow. Why don't you ask Jimmy and Debbie to have breakfast with us Saturday?"

⟞⟝⟞

After breakfast Saturday, Debbie and Jimmy cleared the table. Rachel took a folder out of her tote bag.

"Luke, I want to try something with you."

He nodded.

She pulled out a sheet of paper with four columns of words and laid it in front of Luke.

A	HER	LUKE	SMART
AM	HIS	MY	YOU
AND	I	NAME	YOUR
ARE	IS	NURSE	
DEBBIE	JIMMY	PRETTY	
DOCTOR	LIKE	RACHEL	

"This may seem childish, but humor me," Rachel said. She looked at Luke. "What's your name?"

Luke pointed to LUKE.

"Introduce yourself. Make it a sentence."

Luke studied the words, smiled and pointed MY NAME IS LUKE.

"What is my name?"

YOUR NAME IS RACHEL. Then without prompting he pointed, HIS NAME IS JIMMY. HER NAME IS DEBBIE.

"Yes, yes, you've got it." She pointed to Luke and herself. "What are our professions?"

Luke's hand shook with excitement as it dawned on him what he was doing. YOU ARE A NURSE. I AM A DOCTOR.

"What do you think of Jimmy and Debbie?"

I LIKE JIMMY AND DEBBIE.

"Now," Rachel said, "your final exam. What do you think of me?"

I LIKE...Luke waved his hand, studied the word list, and gave Rachel a mischievous smile. RACHEL IS SMART AND PRETTY.

Rachel hugged Luke. "Oh, I didn't know if you'd remember, or if you'd figure it out if you did. Don't you see? You can't say or write or sign words, but you can select them when you see them. We just need to get you more words."

Luke couldn't quit grinning.

Rachel was pacing back and forth. "Mrs. Cranmore, the English teacher at the high school gave me some ideas." She handed Jimmy and Debbie each a booklet, *Principles of English Grammar,* and described what she wanted them to do. "E-mail your lists. I'll organize them and print them up." She gave Luke a dictionary and several yellow highlighters. "Look up words you use frequently, especially when teaching, and mark them. Jimmy can send them to me."

Jimmy and Debbie chattered enthusiastically as they left.

"Win," Luke said. *Thank you.*

Rachel added "THANK" to the list.

"Say it," she said.

He pointed to the revised list. THANK YOU RACHEL.

With the others working on word lists, Luke was free for the weekend. Since his hymn-singing nonbreakthrough, he had resigned himself to communicating by pointing, pantomime, and through Jimmy. He refused to get excited, or even marginally hopeful, about other communication schemes. Rachel had picked up on much of his and Jimmy's Neanderthal-pantomime system. But this was different. It was so simple. It seemed a little cumbersome, but with practice he was sure it would speed up. Why hadn't anyone thought of it before? Why hadn't he thought of it? This could open new vistas of communication for him. He wouldn't need an interpreter.

He made imaginary rounds with students, searching for words he would need: *what? four steps of a physical exam, anything else? hear, see, feel.*

Rounding with Martin, visiting residents in the afternoon, and searching for words left little idle time. The week flashed by.

The following Saturday, Luke and Jimmy were waiting when Rachel and Debbie finished their shift.

Rachel pulled a chair close to Luke, while Jimmy and Debbie sat on either side. Rachel opened a three-ring plastic notebook filled with pages of word columns in clear plastic pockets.

"A linguist from Georgia Tech helped me organize this. We can modify it if we need to."

She removed the first sheet and placed before Luke. The top half contained in separate boxes: a list of pronouns, the articles *a, an,* and *the,* seven conjunctions, the twenty most common prepositions, the basic punctuation marks, and often-used proper names—Julie, Dr. Martin, Jimmy, Rachel, Helen, and Miss Benson. The rest of this page and the back consisted of, in alphabetical order, the five hundred most commonly used verbs. Pages three and four had the next fifteen hundred verbs. Pages five and six had the fifteen hundred most commonly used nouns, and seven through ten, the next six thousand.

Luke scanned the pages, broke into a huge smile, and gave Rachel thumbs-up. A vocabulary of almost ten thousand words. It would be slow, but much better than his and Jimmy's primitive system.

"This sure beats charades," Jimmy said and handed a page back to Rachel.

Rachel began to gather the pages. "Time to break this up. I need go over lots of stuff with Luke. Jimmy, would it be OK if we commandeered your room for the rest of the day? We need some quiet and privacy."

"Sure," Jimmy said, then laughed. "But no hanky-panky."

Luke grabbed the pages back from Rachel and quickly pointed to *add that.*

"Add what?" Rachel asked.

Luke pointed to *what he said.*

Rachel burst out laughing. "Hanky-panky?" She hit him on the arm. "You dirty old man. I left out all raunchy, salacious, swear, and curse words."

Back in his room, they cleared the bedside table and spread the pages.

"It will speed you up if you highlight the words you use the most. It will be no problem to add words as you need them; we can just reprint the pages." She gave him a blunt plastic stylus. "If you use this, it will be clearer which word you're pointing to. It will also keep the pages cleaner. I won't have my name attached to something smeared with chicken grease."

Luke shook his head. *You've thought of everything.*

They spent the rest of the morning ironing out details. Finally, Luke pointed to *I am hungry. let us go eat.*

"Me, too," Rachel said. "Let me suggest one more thing. It won't have the same flavor and nuance, but it will speed things up a lot."

Luke nodded.

"You've texted and tweeted?"

Another nod.

"Use the same thing here. You can leave out most articles, conjunctions, and prepositions and still get your point across. Everyone is used to that, anyway. For example, instead of 'I am hungry. Let us go eat.' You can indicate, 'Hungry, go eat.'"

When they returned, Rachel said, "I have the whole afternoon free—now talk."

The floodgates were open. He told her about his plans for the medical school. With her gentle prodding, he told her about Julie and her Lucas, his favorite music, most and least favorite foods, and aspects of his life she knew nothing of. By evening, he was much more adept at using his word lists. Rachel knew much more about him, at least the superficial him.

⟫⟨⟨⟩

Like a child with a new toy at Christmas, Luke carried his notebook of word lists at all times, talking with everyone. He and Lily had slow, and often heated, discussions about their latest book. The residents he visited were particularly attracted to it. Their visits were now more two-way. He didn't say much, but he could direct their conversations and ask questions. This allowed him to get to know them even better. He had long sessions with Rachel. He collaborated on cases with Martin in more detail. Jimmy was overjoyed to be able to understand him more fully, but much of the time their old system was quicker. In his spare time, he worked to become more proficient and tried to incorporate the lists into his teaching patterns.

After three weeks, it became increasingly apparent that, while the lists were adequate for leisure communication, it wouldn't work for his needs at the medical school. It wasn't the flop his singing had been. He had become adept at finding words quickly and using shortcuts, but he could talk with only two or three people at a time. They had to be able to see what words he was pointing to. He finally concluded the only way he could be effective was to train someone to function as Jimmy. With the previous system of miming, facial expressions, and body language plus the word lists, he could teach through a surrogate Jimmy. Maybe Martin could get the medical school to send him a trainee. Maybe he couldn't. He lay awake nights stewing about this. He didn't know which would come first, his move to the medical school or his ulcer.

⚎

Luke was sitting in the lobby when Rachel arrived.

"Ready to go?" she asked.

He picked up his notebook and nodded.

"Nervous?" she asked when she parked at the driver's testing station.

He waggled his hand.

"They won't be as tough on you as I have been. You'll do fine."

Forty-five minutes later, Luke drove back into the lot and parallel parked on the first try. When he exited the car, he was beaming. An hour later he had a new driver's license in his wallet.

"Now you can drive back here from Atlanta. We need to celebrate," she said and opened the trunk, revealing a large wicker basket. "In the mood for a picnic?"

He nodded and gave her thumbs-up.

She gave him the keys. "You drive; I'll navigate."

At the exit from the parking lot, he looked at her expectantly. "Take a left."

He began smiling when, three miles down the road, she said, "Turn right on Willow Lane." A couple of minutes later, she instructed, "Slow down. It's not far."

He shushed her and without direction turned into the familiar drive with the sign *Brady Cove.*

"Julie told me you liked to come here. I've been dying to see it," Rachel said when they stopped before an English cottage overlooking the lake. The whole scene had changed little since he moved to Atlanta.

He paid a realty firm in Buxton to maintain the house and yard. Julie and Mark spent weekends and vacations here. Over the years, without Helen's knowledge, he visited when he could slip away. She had never returned. Julie had brought him here twice since he'd come to Shadydale.

The screened sunporch provided a panoramic view of the grounds and lake. Luke set the picnic basket on the table. Rachel leaned on the railing.

"It's lovely. So quiet. So peaceful." She took his hand. "It's too early for lunch. Show me around before we eat."

Walking hand in hand with Rachel transported him back to a time when he and Helen had followed this same course, heard the same bird calls, smelled the same honeysuckle. When Rachel started onto the dock, he pulled back and continued around the edge of the lake. Back on the porch, he tapped on his notebook, *want to see the house?*

"I'd love to," she said.

The furniture was covered with sheets, and a thin sheen of dust clung to everything. The living room opened to a glassed-in eating area affording the same view of the lake and grounds as the sunporch.

"I'd have my morning coffee on the sunporch every day, weather permitting, and here when it was too wet or cold."

The master bedroom had a large window with the same view. He pointed to the bathroom and with his stylus tapped, *it works.*

"Thank you, kind sir. I'll check it out when the tour is complete."

Upstairs, a door on the right side of the landing opened to a large guest bedroom with dormer windows facing the road on one side and the lake on the other. Back on the landing, he made no move to open the other door but started down the stairs. Rachel said nothing.

⇒⇐

Luke emptied the last of the wine into their glasses. He looked at the empty plates and tapped, *if that was a picnic, what is a full dinner like?*

"I'll show you sometime," she said. "However, there's still one course left."

He clapped his hands when she took a key lime pie from a small cooler packed in the basket.

"Julie told me it was your favorite."

———

Luke leaned back, stuffed and contented. When Rachel began clearing the table, he rose to help.

"Just stay seated," she said. "I know where everything goes." Table clear, she set a tote bag in a chair.

"I have a surprise for you, and I wanted to give it to you in a special place." She pointed to the lake. "This is about as special as it gets."

She set two computer tablets before him and stood beside him.

"I knew the original word lists were too slow and limited, but it got you used to the concept and proved it was feasible. We started on this a week after you got the other system."

He leaned forward, uncertain of where this conversation was leading.

"You can thank Mark for this. He and three of his computer guru buddies have been working overtime for the last month to give you time to learn it before going to the medical school. Oh, and thank Helen, too. She paid for it."

Luke tapped, *what is it?*

"This," she pointed to the tablets, "is that," indicating the notebook, "times ten."

She turned them on. The first page of his screen was laid out almost identical to his notebook.

"It's just an expanded touch-screen version of your notebook. You have a working vocabulary of fifty thousand words. If that's not enough," she pointed to two icons, "you can pull up complete standard and medical dictionaries." She turned on the second screen. "When you tap words, they appear on both screens. The person, or persons, you're talking to won't have to look over your shoulder at the notebook."

Luke just stared and tried to absorb all she was saying.

She smiled. "But that's not the best part. Mark checked out the medical school's Wi-Fi. You can transfer information from your screen to the students' laptops. You can talk to a whole class at once."

Luke reached for his tablet.

Rachel gently spanked his wrist. "Or," she continued, "you can e-mail it, tweet it, or text it."

Luke shook his head incredulously.

"Or..." She paused dramatically. "You can hook it to a printer and print it. Luke, you can write again." She let this sink in. "One last thing. Mark says it will take three or four months, but he's convinced he can design a program to have the computer speak the words you put on the screen."

His heart pounded. His fingers trembled as he picked up the stylus.

"Hold it!" she said. "Before you write your first word, be warned. After you go back to the medical school, the first time you go two days without e-mailing me, I'm coming to Atlanta and taking it back. Understand?"

He smiled and nodded, then tapped, *How can I ever thank you?*

Rachel sat across from him and turned the second monitor toward her. She hesitated, then taking his hand in hers, she said, "You can tell me about Lukie—and the real you."

Luke tensed.

"Julie told me you lost a child named Luke. You called him Lukie. She was very vague, no details. I wondered about the collage in your room. Who it was. I've seen the way you look it and how you avoided the dock and his room upstairs. I don't mean to pry, but if I don't understand what happened to you, Helen, and him, I can never begin to understand you."

Luke bit his lip, nodded, and, with a shaky hand, touched the stylus to the screen.

When Lukie died, a great deal of my future died with him...

He began with Lukie's birth, and, in a cathartic release, he tapped for two hours without looking up. Emotionally spent, he tapped, *To be continued.*

Rachel swiped away a tear. "That explains a lot. Thank you for sharing," she said.

They sat silently. Finally, she started to close her tablet. But Luke motioned her to stop. The only sound was the nervous drumming of his stylus on the table. He took a deep breath and with a steady hand tapped, *I love you.*

Rachel stared at the screen and didn't move. Finally, she stood, walked to Luke and tugged his hands. When he stood, she cradled his face in her hands. She gazed up at him. "I love you, too, Luke Brady." She slid her arms around his neck, and standing on tiptoe, gently kissed him.

He paused a moment, then pressed her to him and kissed her passionately.

CHAPTER TWENTY-THREE

L uke had less than six weeks before the move back to Atlanta. For the first time since coming to Shadydale, he was thankful for weekends. He still had breakfast with Rachel and went to church with Jimmy, but committed the rest of his time to teaching preparation. Jimmy and Debbie were seldom around, so he had the room to himself all day Saturday and most of Sunday.

For the first time since Mary's revelations, he was able to speak freely about Lukie's death and his actions. He wrote long letters of apology to Helen and Julie.

His new technology meshed perfectly with his compulsive nature.

He could once again construct elaborate to-do lists and arrangements of the pros and cons of various problems including the move to the medical center. He gave imaginary lectures or teaching rounds from which he extracted extensive lists of: paragraphs introducing each new section of instruction; the most common phrases he used, sorted by anatomic system; new handouts; additions to his old handouts; the most common corrections to a student's physical examination; the most common questions he asked during a student's examination; the answers to the most common questions asked by students. All of this would improve exponentially when he had the speaking program.

He had no doubts he could effectively teach. Who knew? He might become dean again.

⊱⊰

Luke sat in the chapel reviewing the past eight months. His time at Shadydale had been a mixed bag. Benson had been a constant aggravation. On the other hand, he was much better physically. He barely limped when he walked. He used a cane because he could move faster with it. His right hand, though still clumsy with fine motions, was back at full strength. He could feed himself and select words on his tablet with minimal mishaps. His tablet allowed him to interact with others much more normally.

The move to Atlanta would put him nearer Julie and Lucas. Mary's revelations and Helen's departure had eased much of his emotional stress. Everything was looking rosy except for one nagging problem. In his hectic preparation for his move to the medical school, he had given little thought to what he was leaving behind. Jimmy and Debbie had each other and would be fine. But what about Martin? And Lily? And Iron Mike? And all the others? They would be no different than before he came, he told himself.

Most importantly, what about Rachel? He had allowed himself to dream of a life with her. But she wouldn't leave her mother, who might well live several more years. Could their relationship survive on e-mails and sporadic weekend visits?

What if this? What if that? What was the matter with him? It was as if his Calvinist background required something to feel guilty about, even in the midst of good fortune. Why couldn't he just accept it and be happy?

Heeding Father Gabe's advice, he bowed his head and started to pray.

"I saw you sneak in here. Asking God to help you? You pitiful loser, you can't even kill yourself."

He sat bolt upright as Martha's voice shattered his contemplation.

"Yes, I knew about your little escapade within days." She threw up her hands. "Yet here you are, alive and kicking. You're like a damned cat; you have nine lives, and you always land on your feet. You're seeing patients again, thanks to that meddling Dr. Brown. I hate to admit it, but you're good. Now the medical school bigwigs are taking you back to be a hotshot professor. You can't even talk, for Christ's sake. How do you do it?"

He shrugged.

"Going back to screw up someone else's career and life?"

He shook his head and began tapping an apology on his tablet.

"Forget it," she said. "Julie thinks you're a hero again. Even Helen went soft. Before she left for Dallas, I told her about your having the hots for Rachel. She just smiled. Can you believe it? She told Rachel to make you happy."

She pointed a shaky finger at him. "Now it's just you and me, and you've got no lives left. You're not getting out of it this time. Not this time."

She spun about, and shoes squeaking, stalked from the chapel.

Luke sat motionless, all thoughts of God and others forgotten. What did she mean by that? She was becoming more and more unstable. Who knew what she might do next? The lists of pros and cons indicated the move to the medical school was his best option by far. Benson confirmed it. The sooner he got out of here the better.

⊷╬⊶

Rachel and Luke sipped the last of their breakfast coffee. Young Luke made smacking noises as Julie nursed him.

"I swear, I've worried more about this wedding than I did my own," Rachel said.

"I've got Daddy's house spotless," Julie said. "It's a perfect bridal suite. Dinner and breakfast are in the fridge, just need to be stuck into the microwave."

Luke mimed popping a cork.

"Yes, Daddy, the champagne is there, too."

"Be sure and go by the kitchen before you leave," Rachel said. "You won't believe the cake Maybelle fixed. It's huge. Even after the reception, they'll be serving it for the next week." She rechecked her list. "Housekeeping is supposed to set up the chairs early tomorrow morning. I hope the weather's OK."

Relax. Luke tapped on his tablet.

"I know," Rachel said, "I just want everything to be perfect."

"What time do you pick them up Monday morning?" Julie asked.

"After breakfast, around ten. Their flight leaves at two thirty. I hope things go smoothly. Neither Jimmy nor Debbie has ever flown on a plane. Would you believe it—neither has ever been outside of Georgia. But Jimmy was adamant. He said this was their only honeymoon, and they were spending it in Hawaii."

Luke smiled and tapped, *That's my boy.*

⊷⊶

Nothing like this had ever happened at Shadydale. From his vantage point beside Jimmy and Father Ryan, Luke scanned the sun-drenched courtyard. All residents not confined to their beds were shoehorned into folding, wheeled, or tabled chairs on either side of the red carpet running from the dining room door to the kneeling rail at the other end. Iron Mike, resplendent in dress blues, sat in the second row.

The Sunday pianist, armed with a keyboard and a powerful amplifier, presented a medley of songs ranging from Pachelbel's

Canon in D to *Jesu Joy of Man's Desiring* to "When I Fall in Love" to "Till There Was You."

Ushers from the physical therapy staff escorted Julie, Mark, Amy, and Rachel to Jimmy's family seats and the bride's mother, four siblings, and several cousins to seats on the bride's side.

Livingston wheeled Lily to the front and helped her to stand with her walker. Rising to her full four foot eight, she began to sing. "Ave Maria..." Her voice trilled, pure and clear, filling the courtyard, soaring higher and higher. As the last quavering note faded, there was hushed silence.

This was no longer a concrete courtyard, Luke thought. This was holy ground.

The piano began again, and Debbie's sister walked and stood beside Father Ryan. After a brief pause, the opening strains of the wedding march rang out.

Debbie, a vision in white, virtually glowed as she stepped onto the carpet. She smiled at Jimmy. Their gazes locked and never wavered as her father escorted her down the aisle.

"Dearly beloved, we have gathered here today in the presence of God and these witnesses to join this man, James Spencer Jenkins, and this woman, Deborah LeeAnn Watson, in holy matrimony."

After a brief homily on the meaning of marriage, he led them in their vows.

Luke held his breath as Jimmy smoothly intoned, "To have and to hold from this day forward, for better or worse, for richer or poorer, in sickness and in health, till death do us part." Usually his voice reacted as his other muscles, becoming more spastic and jerky when he was stressed. But he had been practicing his vows for weeks, and today delivered them without a glitch.

While they finished their vows and exchanged rings, Luke was seized by misgivings. Could these naive innocents contend with an uncaring outside world for which they had no experience? Would they handle the...*for worse* and...*in sickness* portions of their vows any better than he and Helen had? He prayed they would.

As Jimmy and Debbie knelt, Father Ryan said a prayer and gave a blessing:

> The Lord bless you and keep you,
> The Lord make his face to shine upon you,
> The Lord be gracious unto you
> And give you peace. Amen.

Livingston again helped Lily to her feet. Her voice was barely audible as she began to sing, "Our Father which art in heaven, hallowed be thy name..."

No one stirred. No one cleared his or her throat. It seemed to Luke no one breathed as she continued in a gradual crescendo until, "for thine is the kingdom, and the power, and the glory forever. Amen," reverberated over the audience.

Father Ryan assisted Jimmy and Debbie to stand. He started to speak, but no sound came. He pointed to Lily. "Bless you," he whispered hoarsely.

He cleared his throat. "I now pronounce you husband and wife. What God has joined together, let no man put asunder." He smiled at the couple. "Jimmy, you may kiss your bride."

As they kissed, the crowd burst into spontaneous applause. Luke was surprised to find himself clapping. Was it in appreciation of Lily's celestial singing or for Jimmy and Debbie or just a need to participate in the joy and happiness of the occasion?

Luke scanned the crowd. The only dry eyes he saw belonged to Martha Benson.

CHAPTER TWENTY-FOUR

Martha had fantasized about killing Luke since his admission, but probably had never been serious about it. Besides, as long as he was impounded in Shadydale by a vindictive Helen, it wasn't necessary. In fact, the power to goad him, to prick him, to make him miserable was much more satisfactory. That was about to end. He would be back on top of his world, and she would still be stuck here. That was not going to happen. She had less than three weeks.

She racked her brain for ways to kill him and have it appear to be a natural death. She scoured websites with instructions on how to commit suicide, either self-inflicted or assisted. These all would appear too obvious. How to do it? How to do it? Then one day, while driving home, it hit her. How do people die of strokes? Some die of pneumonia or other infections, some of heart attacks, and some throw clots to their lungs because of inactivity. Most, however, just go to sleep and don't wake up. Everyone assumes they had another stroke and simply quit breathing. What else can make a person quit breathing? She smiled. Of course. She knew just the thing.

Now all she had to do was make it appear a natural death, and cover herself if there was any suspicion it was not.

⊷‖⊶

"Good morning, Rachel," Martha said.

"You're here early today; it's barely five," Rachel said.

Martha began gathering charts. "I need to start preparing for the corporate inspection."

"Are you staying for the party?" Rachel asked.

"What party is that?"

"Dr. Brady's going-away party. He's going back to teach at the medical school in three weeks. There are no vacations this week, so everyone can come."

"I doubt I'll be finished by then." Martha retrieved three more charts. "It's going to be a long day. As soon as I finish, I'm heading home to a hot bath and a good night's sleep."

She puttered around until Rachel left to tend to a patient and then quickly slipped into the medication room. She pulled Luke's box from the medicine cart. It contained a bottle with one blood pressure pill for morning and three bottles of evening medication: four seizure capsules, two antidepressant capsules, and one cholesterol capsule. She pocketed the three evening bottles.

Back in her office, she locked the door and sat at her desk. Pulling a large wad of keys from her pocket, she unlocked the large lower-right desk drawer. Her hands trembled almost beyond her control as she retrieved her supplies: two pills, a mortar and pestle, and a shortened soda straw. Her hands shook as she ground the pills into a fine powder, which she poured onto the glass top of her desk. She pushed the powder into two parallel lines with a six-inch plastic ruler then snorted it up her nose using the straw.

A warm calming glow enveloped her as she rummaged through her treasure trove of narcotics and lifted a twelve-pill blister pack labeled Morphine Sulfate, 100 mg. She hummed a little ditty as she ground these to a talcum powder consistency, which would increase the speed and potency of the medication.

The seven capsules rattled when she dumped them onto the desk. With a steady hand, she pulled them apart, emptied their contents into the wastebasket, and refilled them with the powdered morphine. Her calculation was almost perfect. Only a dusty residue remained in the mortar. She smiled. 1,200 milligrams—wake up in hell, you son of a bitch. She wet her finger and dabbed up the remaining powder. "Ummm," she sighed, and with slow, lingering strokes, she licked the enchanted poppy nectar from her finger.

Judy, the LPN, was the only person at the nurses' station when Martha returned.

"Would you check Mr. Jackson? I thought I heard something as I walked by," Martha said.

When Judy left, Martha placed the bottles with the spiked capsules back into Luke's drawer.

At six, Martha locked her door and walked to the dining room where Amy, Rachel, and several others were decorating and rearranging the tables.

"Looks good," she said. "I'd like to stay, but I'm beat. Oh, Rachel, the party may run late. I hate to ask, but could you oversee the cleanup so things will be ready for breakfast?"

"No problem. Glad to do it," Rachel said.

Martha left smiling. That should keep her occupied while Brady was making his exit.

"Isn't it great!" Jimmy said to Luke. The dining room was festooned with multicolored streamers and balloons. The once three-tiered cake was reduced to a small blob and only a thin sheen of drying milk remained in the ten-gallon ice-cream container.

The spirit of the event infected even the Alzheimer's patients who smiled and laughed as aides wiped crumbs and cream from their faces.

Joe, the unofficial leader of the wheezer geezers, dragged his oxygen tank to Luke's table.

"Doc, we're really sorry to see you go, even if you wouldn't quit ragging our asses about smoking." He motioned to the three puffers behind him. "As a tribute to you, we're all cutting back to a pack a day until you get to Atlanta." They erupted into a chorus of gasping guffaws when he threateningly shook his fist.

Tillie, dressed in her most fashionable outfit, choked back tears and grasped his hand. "Dr. Brady, thank you. I'm going to miss your visits. I enjoy so much talking with you." She placed a pair of knitted mittens on the table. "These will keep your hands warm this winter."

Myrtle, now fully recovered from her pulmonary embolus, kissed his hand. "You saved my life. Thank you."

Sally smiled at him and laid her Raggedy Ann on the table. A few minutes later, she shoved her way back to the head of the line and took it back.

One by one, they filed past, bearing a small gift or sharing a brief moment.

After the room had emptied, Luke, Jimmy, and Martin sat sipping the last of the fruit punch. Rachel walked up to the table with a small tray. "Sorry to break up the party, but it's after ten, and we have to clean up," she said. She sat a small plastic cup with seven capsules before Luke. "Here's your meds for dessert."

Luke washed down the pills with the last of the punch, and they rose to leave.

"I'll see you tomorrow," Martin said. "I need to check a couple of patients, and I'm gone."

"Don't forget your gifts," Rachel said and handed Luke a shopping bag full of knickknacks.

———✥✥———

Jimmy and Debbie walked Luke back to his room. Luke set the sack on the bedside table and slumped into his chair, his face somber.

"They're going to miss you. They love you," Jimmy said.

Luke nodded. *I'm going to miss them.*

"I'm going to miss you, too. I love you, Dr. Brady." Emotion made Jimmy's speech more halting than normal.

"We both love you," Debbie said. She kissed his cheek and hand in hand, she and Jimmy left.

Luke smiled, lay back in his chair and began snoring softly.

———✥✥———

Forty-five minutes later, Rachel came into the room.

"Luke, you dropped one of the mittens Tillie knitted for you." She looked at his slumped form. "Come on, Luke, you need to get out of those clothes and into bed."

No response.

She shook Luke's shoulder. "Come on, Luke, wake up." Still no response. She shook him several more times, and took his vital signs. His blood pressure and pulse were fine, but he was breathing only eight times a minute. She raised his eyelids. When she saw his pinpoint pupils, she dashed to the nurses' station.

"Get Dr. Martin. Quick. Something's wrong with Dr. Brady."

"He just left," the nurses' aide said.

"See if you can stop him."

The aide ran toward the entrance.

"Thank God," Rachel said when Martin came trotting up the hallway.

After a quick examination of Luke, he snapped, "Call nine-nine-one." He turned to Rachel, "He may have had another stroke, but it looks like an overdose."

"Overdose of what? He took his usual dose of Dilantin, Zoloft, and simvastatin. You saw him take them."

"He's barely breathing. Get me an Ambu bag."

Rachel attached the oxygen to the mask, and Martin began to pump.

"Thank goodness," he said, hearing the distant sound of sirens. "We need to get him to the emergency room."

═╬╫═

Luke was again floating, but this time there was no chaotic darkness, just brilliant light. No jumbled confusion, only an overwhelming sense of serenity. He was walking onto the dock behind his home. He had not set foot on it since the day Lukie died. Because of his nightmares, he avoided all bodies of water whenever possible. He stood on the dock, staring over the calm water of the cove. He jerked about at the sound of a loud splash.

His only surprise was his lack of surprise. Lukie straddled the huge black fish as it raced around the cove with porpoise-like leaps and dives; it reminded him of the sculpture of *Boy on a Dolphin* he had seen in London years ago.

Luke waved.

They swam to the dock. Lukie sat astride the fish and looked up at him, unchanged from that last day—the same smile, blue eyes, curly hair. The fish's head protruded from the water chittering at him, its eyes dusky gray, no longer glowing red, its mouth smooth with no jagged piranha teeth.

"It's OK, Daddy. I'm fine."

216

He gave one final smile. As the scene faded, Lukie and the fish slowly turned and swam into the dwindling haze.

⥊⥉⥎

"Dr. Brady. Dr. Brady. Wake up!"

Luke recognized Martin's voice.

"Win." *You don't have to shout.*

"How do you feel?" Martin asked.

Luke smiled and gave him a vigorous thumbs-up. Better than I've felt in a long time. He looked around and raised his eyebrows in a question.

"You're in the emergency room. The drug screen results aren't back, but I'm sure you're full of opiates. You were just about gone. We were going to put you on a ventilator, but after two doses of Narcan, you started breathing better. It's taking a Narcan drip to keep you awake and breathing."

Jimmy sat fidgeting in a metal chair against the wall. Martin shut the treatment room door.

"Rachel called Jimmy. He told me about your suicide attempt."

"I'm sorry, Dr. Brady," Jimmy blurted, "but I thought you might have done it again"

Luke smiled and waved his hand indicating it was OK.

"Did you try again?" Martin asked.

Luke frowned.

"Dr. Brady, did you try to kill yourself again?"

Luke shook his head vigorously.

The door opened and an aide handed Martin a paper.

"God, Dr. Brady...Luke, you're lucky to be alive. Your morphine level is out the roof." He studied the report. "It fits your clinical presentation and response to Narcan, but how could you have gotten morphine?"

"I know," Jimmy said.

CHAPTER TWENTY-FIVE

"Damn." Martha fumbled with the ignition key and dropped it. Her hands trembled as she groped around on the floorboard. She had awakened early and taken her morning Demerol. Ordinarily, she would have taken a second hit by now, but she had stopped at a small bakery for a doughnut and coffee to kill time. She wanted to arrive later than usual and miss the inevitable uproar when Luke was found lifeless. Finally, she found the key. Her hands were shaking so much it took two tries before she could insert it.

Two police cars stood at the entrance to Shadydale. Martha wiped her sweaty palms on her slacks. She really needed a fix. A pill would take at least thirty minutes to take effect. She needed to be calm and have her wits about her. She'd shoot some Demerol IV as soon as she got to her office.

She hesitated when she saw the lights were on in her office. The door swung open before she could unlock it.

"Sheriff Collins. Is there a problem?" she said, feigning surprise.

"I'm afraid there is," he said.

"What is it?"

"Dr. Brady."

"What happened? Did he have another stroke?"

"Let's go down to the conference room."

"There's something I must do first. I'll be right down," Martha said and tried to push past him.

He stood his ground. "It can wait." He shut the door to her office and motioned to one of the deputies who took his position at the door. Another accompanied him and Martha.

Martin, Amy, Rachel, and Jimmy sat in chairs outside the conference room. Collins ushered her in.

"What's going on?" Martha asked, her voice rising.

"Please sit down," Collins said. When she sat, he continued. "Last night, Dr. Brady received a massive overdose of morphine."

"Oh no!" Martha gasped. "How is he?"

"He almost died, but he's fine."

"How did he get morphine?" Martha asked. *Damn him! He landed on his feet again.*

"That's what we want to find out," Collins said. "Amy assures me the narcotics count is accurate, and all narcotics are accounted for. "Where could he have gotten morphine?"

"He must have been saving them. You know he tried to kill himself several months ago," Martha said. Her heart pounded and perspiration beaded her forehead.

"Dr. Brown assures me he hasn't prescribed morphine for Dr. Brady since he's been here. In fact, he's not ordered morphine for anyone for over a week."

"Rachel must have made a mistake," Martha said.

"Perhaps, but the pharmacist is certain the proper amount of all other medications was delivered yesterday morning. He's re-checked the pill count, and it is accurate. Did he make a mistake, too?"

"How should I know? I wasn't even here last night." Her stomach cramped. She felt as if her whole body was vibrating. She needed a fix.

Collins continued without pause. "I saw in your personnel record you've had problems with narcotics."

"That was a long time ago," Martha said through gritted teeth. "I went through rehab."

"It's supposed to be in the nineties today. I notice you're wearing long sleeves. The staff tells me you always wear long sleeves. Would you mind rolling them up?"

Martha crossed her arms. "No, and you better not touch me."

"We can address that later if we need to," Collins said.

"I told you. I went through rehab. I'm clean."

"I understand." He motioned to the deputy. "Jim, would you bring Mr. Jenkins in."

Jimmy stood shifting from one foot to the other.

"Please sit down, Mr. Jenkins. Would you tell me about the incident in Miss Benson's office?"

Jimmy stared at the table, avoiding eye contact with Martha.

"Don't be nervous. Just tell us what you saw."

Jimmy sat, eyes downcast. "I...I..." he stammered.

"Just tell us what you saw. It's important," Collins said.

Jimmy took a deep breath. "I went to see Miss Benson because someone stole my newspaper three days in a row. I just walked in. I know I should have knocked, but I was so mad." He hesitated.

"Go on," Collins said.

"Miss Benson was injecting something in her arm. When she saw me, she threw a bottle and the syringe into her desk drawer."

She sprang to her feet, pointed to Jimmy, and screamed, "You suspect me because of something that spastic retard said. He's lying. Why didn't he say something then?"

"Why didn't you tell Dr. Brown or someone, Mr. Jenkins?" Collins asked.

"I was scared of her. She said she would throw me out of Shadydale if I told anyone. Where would I go? What would I do?"

"Do you remember which drawer she threw them in?" Collins asked Jimmy.

"Yes, sir, the big drawer on the bottom right side."

"Why don't we go down to your office, and you can clear all of this up?" Collins said.

"You can't just go poking around in my office. There are privileged items there. It's...it's...it's not legal."

Collins handed her a piece of paper. "This search warrant says it's quite legal."

He rose and opened the door. "Dr. Martin, Mr. Jenkins, Mrs. Maxwell, Mrs. Graham, will you come with Mrs. Benson and me to the office."

"You have no right to do this," Martha protested.

"Mrs. Benson, don't make this any more difficult than it needs to be." He gently took her arm and led her out.

The deputy held the door as they entered Martha's office.

"Jack, don't let anyone else in. And," he added, "detain that administrator, Crandell, when he gets here."

Collins pushed the desk chair to Martha. "Please sit down," he said and motioned for Martin, Amy, Rachel, and Jimmy to sit on the couch.

"Would you please give me the key to the desk, Mrs. Benson?"

Her hands trembled as she slid the key off the ring and handed it to him.

He opened the drawer. It was over half-full of blister packs, bottles of various pills, and numerous vials of liquid medication.

"Jack, get the DEA down here to catalog these." He turned to Amy. "If the narcotics counts have been accurate, where could these have come from?"

"I don't know. Narcotics are kept in the pharmacy or locked in the safe in the nurses' station."

"How could they have been removed if the narcotics count was accurate?"

Amy shifted uneasily. "If someone falsified the records."

"How could that happen?" he continued.

"The easiest way would be to list a medication as given to a patient but not give it."

"When the DEA comes, you'll need to help them reconcile as much of this as you can with your records," Collins said.

Martha slumped into her chair and began sobbing. "I'm so sorry. I just couldn't help myself. I need help."

Collins ignored her as he slipped on rubber gloves, picked up the wastebasket and put it on the desk.

Martha's heart pounded even stronger. How could she have been so stupid? Why hadn't she emptied it last night?

He rummaged through the wastebasket, dropping its contents on the desktop. Finally, he came to a blister pack labeled Morphine Sulfate 100 mg. with twelve empty blisters. He placed it in a clear evidence bag.

"Is this used here at Shadydale?" Collins asked Martin.

"Yes," Martin said, "but only with a signed, written physician's order."

"Would this have been enough to cause Dr. Brady's problem?" Collins persisted.

"Yes," Martin said. "With that amount, I can see how Dr. Brady almost died."

Collins picked the rest of the trash from the wastebasket. "Hmm," he murmured. He handed a plastic evidence bag to the deputy. "Could you hold this for me?" He then lifted the basket and poured the powdery residue at the bottom into the bag.

"Dr. Martin, what should I have the lab check this for?" he asked.

"Dr. Brady was on Dilantin, Zoloft, and simvastatin," Martin said.

Collins made a note on the bag.

"Mrs. Graham, would you go get Dr. Brady's medication box?" he said.

Sweat dripped from Martha's chin onto her blouse. She clasped her hands together in a vain attempt to control her trembling. "Are you blind?" she said. "Can't you see they're all trying to set me up?"

Collins silently studied Martha's certificates until Rachel returned.

"Who dispenses the medications from this box?" he asked Martha.

"Amy on the day shift and Rachel at night," Martha said.

"Do you ever dispense medicines?"

"Occasionally, when we're shorthanded."

"Did you give Dr. Brady his medications last night?"

"No! I already told you I wasn't even here last night. I left before his stupid party," Martha said in a higher key.

Collins persisted. "When was the last time you gave Dr. Brady his medicines?"

"I don't remember. It had to be weeks ago—maybe months."

"I see," Collins said. Very carefully he placed the four bottles in an evidence bag. "So how would you explain it if the lab finds your fingerprints on these bottles?"

Martha sat bolt upright and glared first at Collins then at Martin, Amy, Rachel, and Jimmy. "You sanctimonious hypocrites. You're as bad as Brady. You'll be sorry, I promise you." She turned back to Collins. "I'm not answering any more of your questions. I want a lawyer."

"I think you need one," Collins said. "The DEA and the Georgia Board of Nursing will deal with the narcotics. The Georgia Bureau of Investigation is investigating you and Cantrell for fraud in the illegal appropriation of funds in the case of two hundred mattresses and covers."

"Crandell made me do that," she said.

"Maybe so, but you have far more pressing matters to deal with," Collins said.

"What do you mean?" Martha asked.

Collins took out his handcuffs. "Martha Benson, you are under arrest for the attempted murder of Dr. Luke Brady. You have the right to remain silent. Anything you say can and will be used against you—"

The rest was drowned out by Martha's sobs.

CHAPTER TWENTY-SIX

Morning rounds completed, Luke picked at his lunch.
"Hi, Dr. Brady."

Luke spun around at Jimmy's voice. *Sit down*, he motioned.

"I'm sorry I haven't been to see you, but I've been so busy. So much is happening," Jimmy said.

Luke gave a quizzical look.

"Amy talked to the owners, and they're going to give me a trial as bookkeeper for Shadydale."

Luke smiled and clapped him on the shoulder.

"We don't need the money, but this gives me something to do while Debbie finishes nursing school." He began tearing Luke's napkin in small pieces. "I'm a little scared. I've never had a real job before."

Luke pointed at him and held up the OK sign.

"And I can still see my other friends here." He wadded the napkin and pushed it aside. "There's more. We've bought a house. It's only a block and a half away. We move in Tuesday."

Forgetting himself, Luke blurted, "Win!" *That's great, Jimmy; you deserve a load of happiness.* He then quickly tapped it on the tablet.

"We'd like to show it to you. Could you have lunch with us next Sunday?"

Beaming, Luke nodded.

"Debbie will pick you up and show you where it is."

After a few more minutes, Jimmy rose. "Got to go; I have to help pick out carpet." He laughed and pointed to the tile floor. "I haven't walked on carpet in fourteen years. I hope I don't fall."

The dining room was now empty.

"Could I get you something, Dr. Brady?" the aide asked.

He smiled and made a T with his hands. She returned with a cup of hot tea.

More pensive now, he sipped his tea. *Jimmy, you deserve whatever good comes to you. If Lukie had lived, I'd want him to be like you—kind, thoughtful, determined, industrious.* His cup stopped midway to his mouth. *You're the same age Lukie would have been. You're more than a friend; you're like a surrogate son.* His mind flashed back to his suicide attempt.

"You're the only father I've ever known," Jimmy had said.

Luke smiled. Jimmy had realized it long before he did.

⟨⟩

Debbie and Luke sat in the living room as Jimmy cleared the table.

"He insists on helping," she said. "I just hope it lasts."

Luke laughed and tapped, *I bet it will.*

They had spent the last four hours reviewing the past year and looking at pictures from the wedding and Hawaiian honeymoon.

"We're going to miss you, Dr. Brady, all of us, but especially Jimmy. I know it's an hour's drive from Atlanta to here, but we'll come get you whenever you can visit. You can use the extra bedroom and stay as long as you like."

Luke nodded uncertainly.

After another hour, Luke rose and tapped, *This has been wonderful, but I must go.*

"I wish you could stay longer," Debbie said.

Luke took them both in his arms.

Debbie kissed him on the cheek. "Thank you so much for coming. Visit us often. Please."

I may visit more than you suspect, he tapped.

At the end of the street, before Debbie could turn toward Shadydale, Luke pointed to the left.

"Would you like to go somewhere?" she asked.

Luke nodded and pointed.

Following his instructions, she drove toward Buxton and finally entered Buxton Memorial Gardens. He directed her to a spot in the back corner of the cemetery.

He motioned for them to follow him. Using his cane, he walked carefully up the slope and stopped at a stone marker flanked by two benches and two large cedars. The inscription read, LUCAS WINSTON BRADY. This was his first visit in almost a year.

No one spoke for several minutes.

"He was your little boy?" Debbie said.

Luke nodded.

"He was born the same year as me," Jimmy said. "I didn't know that."

They stood in uneasy silence.

Near tears, Debbie's voice was husky. "I'm so sorry. Would you like some time alone?"

He nodded.

"Take as long as you need," she said. "We'll meet you at the car." She took Jimmy's hand. "Show me your mother's grave."

Luke sat on the nearest bench. Dancing flickers of sunlight splashed through a canopy of leaves agitated by a balmy September breeze, laden with the scent of honeysuckle. Small gray-and-yellow finches chattered and flitted from branch to branch.

He allowed his mind to wander through a medley of memories of times before *that* day. Without warning, lines from a long-forgotten poem intruded on his reverie: *Of all the words of tongue and pen, these are the saddest, it might have been.*

"That's some heavy material."

"It slipped up on me," Luke said, not surprised at Gabe's appearance. "I try to avoid those things that should have been but never were. They can drive you crazy."

Gabe sat on the bench beside him.

"I saw Lukie," Luke said.

"That's great. When?"

"While I was snockered on morphine. I heard of people having visitations from lost loved ones. I prayed for something like that for years. Do you have to nearly die to get a prayer answered?"

"Listen to yourself. You get what you want, and you complain about the circumstances. A little gratitude might be in order."

Luke winced. "You're right. What's the matter with me?" He stared at the ground. "He never had a chance to accomplish anything, to make a difference. I'd like to make a difference for him."

"Good idea," Gabe said.

"But how?"

"Hey, in less than a month you get to start your life over again. Not many people have such an opportunity."

"How does that make a difference?"

"You get to inspire several generations of new physicians. And didn't I hear they planned to do a documentary about you?"

"Yes," Luke said.

"Wouldn't that be an inspiration for stroke victims everywhere?"

"Perhaps," Luke said.

"You got something against being a success? Being admired? Hasn't that been your goal for the last twenty years?"

Luke sighed. "God forgive me, yes."

"That's not what you want?"

Luke clenched and unclenched his fists. "Not anymore."

"Why not?" Gabe persisted.

"I once told you my life's mission statement was to live for God first, family second, medicine third, and me last."

"I remember; that's an admirable plan."

"I've done a lot of thinking lately. I said the right things, but I lived it exactly backward, especially after Lukie died."

"And…?"

"You said I had a chance to start my life over again. I think you're right. I've already had two. I survived a stroke and an overdose, both of which should have killed me. I think there's a message there. The place to start over is not at the medical school. If I go back to the medical school, I'll reverse it again. I know I will. It will be me first—impressing my colleagues and students—medicine second, and maybe a little something left over for family and God. You told me to talk with your boss. I did. And I listened. My goal has always been to do something big. After a lot of thought, I believe I'm better doing little things that help. I'm convinced I was put in Shadydale for a purpose. If I get this right, the rest might fall into place: my family—Julie, Rachel, Jimmy, the lonely residents; medicine with Martin; and me, last."

"If not the medical school, then where?" Gabe asked.

"At Shadydale."

"Shadydale. That monotonous, smelly hellhole? Did you run this through one of your pros and cons exercises?"

"As a matter of fact, I did," Luke said.

"What did you conclude?"

"The smart thing for me to do is return to the medical school."

"So…?"

"It would be the smart thing, but not the right thing. The right place for me is here."

"At Shadydale. You've got to be kidding. What about being an inspiration to generations of new physicians and stroke victims everywhere?"

"The medical students have scores of mentors to inspire them. What about those lonely people with few sources of help and inspiration?" Luke said.

"And that would be at Shadydale?"

"Yes, Shadydale. Most of the residents never have a visitor. They're all alone. I've seen what a little personal attention can do for them. Maybe that's why I was put there."

"But they're here for the duration, on a downhill course to the cemetery regardless of what you do."

"Father, you might be a priest, but you don't understand anything. They need someone to just be there, someone to listen, someone to care. I can do that."

Gabe smiled and held up his hands. "Easy, Luke, I'm with you. I just want you to be certain."

"I'm pretty sure. I think I'm probably certain," Luke said and then burst into laughter at Gabe's startled look.

"OK, I'm as certain as I can be," he said.

"The medical school won't like this at all. They're not likely to make this offer again," Gabe said.

"I know. I've talked with them. Maybe, if they think the students need me to inspire them, they'll start rotating students through Shadydale again."

"So you're comfortable with your decision."

"No, I'm not comfortable, but I'm getting there. I think it's the right one."

Gabe stood, laid his hand on Luke's shoulder, and looked him directly in the eye. "You've come a long way, Luke. I'm sure you'll make Lukie proud."

"Thank you," Luke said. "Thank you for everything." He paused. "Will I see you again?"

"I don't know. I hope so."

"Me too," Luke said.

He started to walk away.

"Wait," Luke said.

Gabe turned back. "What is it?"

"Who...what are you? Are you real?"

"Am I real to you?"

"Yes, but..."

"But what? Does it make any difference?"

Luke thought for a moment and smiled. "No, I guess not."

Gabe smiled, held up his hand as in a blessing, then turned and walked away.

Now alone, Luke knelt by the marker. He gently brushed away clinging grass clippings from the last mowing. His vision blurred. *I miss you so much, Lukie.* He sniffed and cleared his throat.

Retrieving his cane, he stood to go, but he stopped after a few steps. Something drew him back to the marker. His intent gaze crept over every square inch. Except for a slight weathered darkening, it stood unchanged from the day it was erected, no different from his many previous visits. What was it? Unable, or unwilling, to move, he stared, more perplexed with each passing second. He gave a sudden, involuntary gasp, followed by a spreading smile. He stumbled back to the marker and once more knelt before it. Still smiling, he placed his finger in the recessed W of the inscription and with great care began to trace the first three letters. "Win," he said.

The End

84159337R00132

Made in the USA
Lexington, KY
21 March 2018